COOPER'S CORNER CHRONICLE

Doc McAlester Ties the Knot

Anyone who's spent time in our little town soon discovers there are no secrets in Cooper's Corner. Dr. Alex McAlester tried his best to keep his wedding to Jenny Taylor under wraps, but our super snoopers found out the time (late yesterday afternoon) and place (Church of the Good Shepherd). Headed by Philo and Phyllis Cooper, a party of well-wishers was at the church doors to greet the newlyweds.

The bride and groom and their witnesses, Grace and Tuck McCabe and Maureen Cooper, were whisked off to Philo and Phyllis's home for a potluck in their honor. Of course, the question on everyone's mind was how our busy vet managed to carry on a long-distance romance with his new bride when she was living in New York. Apparently that's one secret the newlyweds intend to keep to themselves.

Cooper's Corner residents wish Jenny and Alex all the best in their marriage. It was only a short time ago that we bid a sad farewell to Ed Taylor, Jenny's dad and a beloved member of the community. Jenny must miss her father on such a happy occasion, but we all know Ed would have given this marriage his fondest blessing.

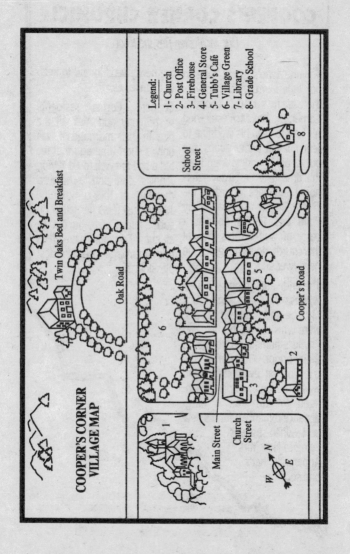

COOPER'S CORNER
VILLAGE MAP

Twin Oaks Bed and Breakfast

Oak Road

Cooper's Road

School
Street

Church
Street

Main Street

Legend:
1- Church
2- Post Office
3- Firehouse
4- General Store
5- Tubb's Café
6- Village Green
7- Library
8- Grade School

W E N S

COOPER'S CORNER

DEBBI RAWLINS

For Better or for Worse

HARLEQUIN®

TORONTO • NEW YORK • LONDON
AMSTERDAM • PARIS • SYDNEY • HAMBURG
STOCKHOLM • ATHENS • TOKYO • MILAN • MADRID
PRAGUE • WARSAW • BUDAPEST • AUCKLAND

HARLEQUIN BOOKS
225 Duncan Mill Road, Don Mills,
Ontario, Canada M3B 3K9

ISBN 0-373-61261-3

FOR BETTER OR FOR WORSE

Debbi Rawlins is acknowledged as the author of this work.

Dear Reader,

You must be getting pretty familiar with the townsfolk of Cooper's Corner by now. I sure am. Writing a book for a continuity series is quite an experience—mostly pleasant, but sometimes mind-boggling. And frustrating. But the finished story is always worth the effort.

It's a challenge to work with continuing characters, but I had fun discovering how they were depicted by other authors in the series. And of course it's always a pleasure to write about new romances.

I sure love my job! And I hope you enjoy being part of Alex and Jenny's growing relationship.

Debbi Rawlins

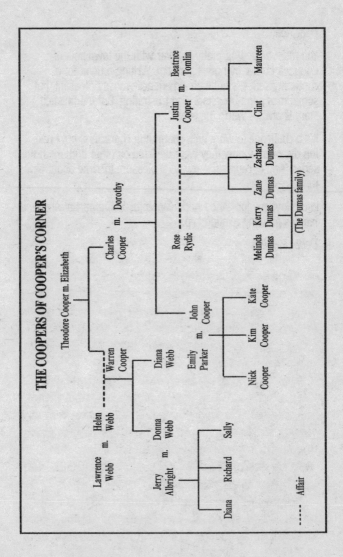

THE COOPERS OF COOPER'S CORNER

Theodore Cooper m. Elizabeth

Lawrence Webb m. Helen Webb ------ Warren Cooper

Charles Cooper m. Dorothy

Justin Cooper m. Beatrice Tomlin

Clint   Maureen

Rose Rydic ------

Zane Dumas   Zachary Dumas

Melinda Dumas   Kerry Dumas

(The Dumas family)

Donna Webb   Diana Webb

John Cooper m. Emily Parker

Nick Cooper   Kim Cooper   Kate Cooper

Jerry Albright m.

Diana   Richard   Sally

------ Affair

CHAPTER ONE

ALEX MCALESTER squinted at the kitten through the branches of the oak tree, amazed that the little guy had gotten so high. Alex's jeans caught on a jagged piece of bark, and he grunted. Even more amazing was the fact that he'd managed to drag his poor forty-year-old bones halfway up the trunk.

"Now, don't you two fret." Phyllis Cooper stood on the sidewalk in front of the general store, consoling Maureen Cooper's twins, her charges for the afternoon. "This is nothing for Dr. McAlester. He treats ornery bulls and even tended a sick tiger when the circus came to town five years back. He'll get that kitten down in no time. You'll see."

Alex glanced at the kids' anxious faces and sighed. Gee, no pressure here. He shinnied up another foot, ignoring the scrapes to his arms. The kitten was obviously frozen scared and the only way he was going to come down was if someone carried him.

"Doc Alex? You won't let the kitty fall, will you?" one of the twins asked.

He glanced down and met large blue-green eyes. He couldn't tell if it was Randi or Robin—they looked too much alike. Not that it mattered. Both little girls gazed at him with a mixture of trust and concern that made his gut tighten.

"Don't worry, honey, I'll get the kitty down safely. You just be really quiet so we don't frighten him, okay?"

Both girls promptly nodded.

What would his life have been like if he and Sara had had a couple of children, if they hadn't postponed starting a family? They'd always assumed there would be time later. They'd been horribly wrong.

But he couldn't afford to think about that now. The kitten let out a plaintive meow, and Alex inched up the last couple of feet until he could reach the gray tabby. Alarmed, the cat struck out and clawed his arm, but Alex managed to grab him.

"Easy, boy," he said in a low, soothing voice. "I know you're scared, but we're going to get your feet planted on the ground again."

The kitty didn't believe him. He screeched and squirmed, and Alex had to tuck him inside his shirt to free his hands for the climb down. The cat dug into Alex's skin. He winced but continued another couple of yards until he was able to hand the nervous animal to Phyllis.

"Be careful," he warned. "The poor guy's spooked. He'll try to claw you, so hold him by the back of his neck."

Phyllis didn't seem to be listening. Something across the street had distracted her. Absently, she held up her hands for the kitten.

"Phyllis?"

She squinted in the direction of the bank as she took the cat. "Isn't that Jenny Taylor?"

Damn it. Alex nearly slid the last few feet to the ground. "Who?"

"You know, Ed's daughter?"

He knew who she was. He just hadn't expected her to arrive until this evening. As soon as he landed on his feet, he peered across the street. Her back was to him, her long, light cinnamon-colored hair pulled into a ponytail.

"Of course, she's come for the funeral. I don't think I've seen her in over five years." Phyllis frowned in disapproval. "Too bad she didn't come see her father when he was alive. Guess she's been too busy living the high life in Boston."

"New York," he mumbled, craning his neck for a better look and tucking his loose T-shirt into his jeans. "She got transferred there two years ago."

He doubted Jenny had been living the high life, but he didn't say anything. Phyllis would only argue. She and her husband, Philo, had owned Cooper's Corner General Store for over three decades and knew just about everyone in town. They both pretty much figured they knew everyone's business, too. Probably did.

Except Alex knew all about Jenny, even though he hadn't seen her in years. Her father had read him every one of her letters chronicling her ten-year career in the hotel industry, from her first job as assistant to the general manager to her present position as head of the marketing department in the chain's newest boutique hotel in New York.

Ed had been proud of each of his daughter's promotions and worried sick when she'd broken her leg skiing in Vermont three winters ago. Hell, as Ed's closest neighbor and best friend, Alex knew when Jenny had had a cold. Damn, he was going to miss the guy. Only fifty-seven and dead from a sudden heart attack. It wasn't right.

Sara had only been thirty when cancer had claimed her young life.

Alex ruthlessly pushed the thought aside. He needed to focus on Jenny. She wouldn't be prepared for what she'd find at the house where she'd grown up. Ed hadn't had the heart to tell her about the hard times that had hit the farm. He'd been unable to make ends meet, and the place was old and had started to require extensive repair.

Alex had found out by accident that Jenny had been sending Ed money until two years ago. But then it stopped, and Ed had been too proud to accept Alex's offer of help. Now all Alex could do was offer Jenny a shoulder to lean on. He owed Ed that much.

He kept his sights on her as he waited for an old van and an SUV to go by before crossing Main Street. Jenny stopped briefly at a mailbox, deposited an envelope and turned to climb into a blue sedan. It was an older car with a dent in the door. Not what he'd expected her to be driving. He figured something newer, sportier would be more her style.

Of course a car didn't mean anything. He had a

thriving veterinary practice, busy enough that he'd taken on a partner. Yet he still drove the same ugly ten-year-old truck he and Sara had picked out a year before she'd died.

Anyway, he was more interested in the direction the car was pointed. She'd been heading toward Church Street when she came into town, which meant she probably hadn't been to the farm yet. Better he was with her when she stepped inside the house. Ed had gotten used to the state of disrepair. Alex doubted Jenny would be as indifferent.

But maybe he was wrong. She hadn't visited her father in quite a while, always claiming she was too busy with work. Ed never said much, only that he was proud of her becoming such a success. The poor guy must have felt neglected, though. Alex had tried to reserve judgment, but it was hard to ignore the disappointment in Ed's eyes as each holiday approached and Jenny made no effort to come home.

Her past visits normally lasted just two days…a long weekend. But Ed was grateful for every minute. She was his only daughter, his only living relative. And now he was gone, and Jenny wouldn't have any more chances to visit him.

None of that mattered to Alex at the moment. Even if he did feel any ill will toward Jenny for her apparent neglect of her father, he'd never let her suffer the trauma of the next two days alone. Alex understood the devastation of loss all too well.

A delivery truck pulled out from the curb and blocked his way. By the time he got across the street,

Jenny had driven away, headed toward the farm. Luckily his pickup was parked just in front of him.

"Hey, Alex, where are you going?" Phyllis called, hands on her hips. She'd passed the kitten to one of the twins. "What are we supposed to do with this little fellow?"

He sighed. They'd called him to get the cat down. Silly him for figuring they knew the owner or had a game plan once they got a hold of the kitten. "Hang on to him for a while. I'll be back later."

"But—"

Alex jumped into his pickup and started the engine. Phyllis had to be going nuts wondering what had gotten into good ol' dependable Doc McAlester. She'd get over it. Jenny Taylor was his concern.

JENNY PULLED into the drive and parked in front of the eighteen-fifties New England farmhouse where she had lived most of her life. She barely recognized the place.

The peeling paint wasn't the worst of the neglect and disrepair. Two of the shutters were gone, while another pair hung loosely from its hinges. The roof was missing enough shingles that the ceiling had to leak inside. The place looked abandoned. Yet her father had lived here until his death four days ago.

Why hadn't he told her he was in this much trouble? They talked twice a week. He'd mentioned grain prices had gone up, and she knew that wet weather had cut last year's harvest in half, but she'd had no idea the farm was in jeopardy. He'd been so proud of the growing market for the free-range chickens he'd raised. His reputation was spreading, and he could hardly keep up with the demand. But obviously his earnings had been much less than she'd imagined.

Jenny stayed in the driver's seat, laid her head back and closed her eyes. He should have confided in her. Although she couldn't have done anything about it. She was flat broke. Not just broke, but in debt. Without a job. And soon she'd have no place to live.

Slowly she opened her eyes and stared again at the house. "Oh, Dad," she whispered. "What happened?"

She'd failed him. That's what had happened. She'd planned to go off into the world, be a huge success, save the farm he loved so much. But it was too late.

Before despair swallowed her whole, she opened the car door and forced her feet to the ground, needing to do something that would distract her from the destructive thoughts threatening her sanity. If she'd learned nothing else in therapy, negative thinking was the surest way to sink quickly into depression and hopelessness.

Tomorrow was her father's funeral. She had to be prepared both emotionally and physically. After grabbing the small bag of groceries she'd brought, she made her way to the front door, mindful of the rickety wooden steps leading to the porch. The same rocker she'd played on as a child sat in the corner. Only she wouldn't dare trust it to hold her now. A couple of back slats were missing, and one of the arms had partially rotted away. The chair should have been discarded long ago.

Jenny opened the front door. It wasn't locked. It never was. Not here in Cooper's Corner. How different life was from the frantic pace of Boston and Manhattan. At one time those cities had seemed glamorous and exciting. Not anymore. And anyway, she had neither the resources nor the energy to enjoy the fast-paced lifestyle. These days, getting out of bed required all her strength. And then all she could do was sit on her couch and worry about money.

Sighing, she made her way over the threshold, only partly prepared for what waited inside. The sight of warped floorboards and torn drapes made her stomach sink. Her father's blue recliner had faded to a dull gray.

The place was spotless, though, except for a little dust. The rugs looked clean, the floor swept and the oak table her grandfather had made over seventy years ago was polished to a shine. On the mantel was the familiar row of photos...her parents' wedding day, her mother a month before her death, when Jenny was two. The rest of the photos were of Jenny, ranging from infancy to college graduation.

She picked up her senior high school picture and smiled at the studious-looking girl in brown-framed glasses. Her eyesight had been as perfect then as it was now, but she'd always looked young for her age, and with her freckled nose, she'd felt she needed the glasses to enhance her maturity.

Of course, everyone in Cooper's Corner had known

everything about her, anyway—the boys she dated, the year she'd been stood up for the prom and was too humiliated to go to school for an entire week.

There were no secrets in a small town. That's why she'd had to get away. Go someplace where she could succeed or fail without it being fodder for the patrons of the local beauty shop or Tubb's Café.

Had it been worth it, she wondered as she made her way to the kitchen and set down the sack of groceries. The linoleum floor was more yellow than white, but clean nevertheless, as were the Formica countertops. She thought briefly about putting the perishable groceries in the fridge, but figured she'd better check out the rest of the house first. As limited as her budget was, she didn't know if she could stay here.

She didn't mind the shabbiness, but the memories and guilt sluiced over her like scalding water. If she'd swallowed her pride and come home, would things have turned out differently?

Now she'd never know. Taking a deep shuddering breath, she left the groceries and headed down the hall toward her room. Not much had changed. Her dresser was still there, and her old twin bed with the white lace canopy, which had begun to shred years ago.

She started over the threshold to test the condition of the mattress, but one of the floorboards buckled under her feet and she nearly landed on her fanny. Holding the doorframe for support, she backed into the hall. She'd try her father's room. Surely it was in better shape.

Updated with what appeared to be a fresh coat of light blue paint, the master bedroom was in decent enough condition to be a relief. The ugly plaid drapes that hung on the windows made her smile.

Every trip home she pleaded with her father to let her replace them, but he would always refuse, telling her to go buy herself a nice new outfit instead. She'd end up buying groceries and stocking his pantry for winter.

She stared at the hideous brown plaid, the back of her eyes beginning to sting. Damn, she wished she'd changed the curtains.

A loud knock startled her. It sounded as if it came from the back door. Dabbing at the stray tear on her cheek, she retraced her steps to the kitchen, this time watchful of any loose floorboards.

Through the screen she could see a man, tall, really tall, and broad-shouldered, ash-blond hair, but the glare of the afternoon sun made it impossible to make out his face.

"Jenny? It's Alex McAlester."

She peered closer. "Dr. McAlester?"

"You probably don't remember me."

"Of course I do." She pushed open the screen as he stepped back and caught the door. "You have the vet practice down the road a couple of miles. Dad spoke of you often."

Dr. McAlester's expression saddened. "Yeah, I'm going to miss him." His warm gray eyes met hers. "I'm sorry, Jenny. Your dad was a great guy."

She nodded, unable to speak, and motioned him inside.

"I'd hoped to be here when you arrived." He gave her a faint smile. "But I got waylaid in town."

"That's all right. I didn't expect anyone to be here." She stepped back when she realized she blocked his way. Truthfully, she'd rather be alone, but Dr. McAlester had been a good friend to her father, and he was grieving, too.

He had to duck when he entered the kitchen. He must be six five or thereabouts, yet oddly, he didn't seem as tall as she remembered. Of course, she'd been so young the last time she'd seen him, he'd probably looked like a giant to her. Especially since she hadn't shot up to five seven until she was nearly twenty.

"It's good to see you, Jenny. What's it been, about nine, ten years?"

At the censure in his voice, she stiffened. Or maybe it was her guilty conscience. "I was home for a visit a year and a half ago."

He nodded, his expression unreadable. "I know. A lot has changed since then."

She swallowed. "I've noticed." She turned away and went to the cupboard. "I'll make some coffee." No doubt she'd find a large supply. Her dad would go without food rather than be deprived of coffee.

Dr. McAlester automatically picked up the coffee carafe and filled it with water while she ground the beans. They worked in silence for a few minutes, lost in their own thoughts.

Maybe it was good that Dr. McAlester had shown

up. He probably knew her dad better than anyone. She'd find out what had happened, why her dad had let the place get so run-down. Maybe she'd even be able to ignore the guilt pricking her conscience. At least for a while.

"How do you take your coffee?" she asked as she opened the refrigerator door and realized there was no cream.

"Black." He used his chin to indicate the cupboard where the mugs were kept. "There's some powdered creamer in there if that's what you're looking for.

Annoyed that he knew the kitchen better than she did, Jenny got down the creamer and two mugs. She placed them on the oak table that had been in the family since before she was born, then stopped when she realized her father hated powdered creamer. If you didn't have the real stuff, it wasn't worth drinking the coffee, he used to say often enough.

Dr. McAlester pulled out one of the chairs, and she looked into his gentle smile. "He switched to the powder because it was cheaper. You know your dad, always practical."

Jenny blinked away the threat of tears and sank into the chair he continued to hold for her. She cleared her throat, hoping her voice was still serviceable. "What happened?" she whispered.

When he didn't respond right away, she figured he hadn't heard her, but he sat across the table from her, finding and holding her gaze, and she knew she was about to hear the unvarnished truth.

"A year ago, your father had a balloon payment

due on the farm. It took most of his savings to pay
it off.''

She shook her head. ''That's not possible. He
owned the farm free and clear.''

Surprise flickered in his eyes. ''He took a loan out
against the property five years ago.''

''But he would have told me.''

Dr. McAlester didn't say anything. He looked
away, then got up to get their coffee.

She didn't jump up to help as she'd normally do.
She was too numb. Why hadn't her father confided
in her? Five years ago, she had been in a good position to help financially. She'd sent him money,
which he'd tried to turn down, and when he ripped
up her checks, she'd resorted to money orders. If
she'd known he had a big loan to repay, she would
have forced him to accept more.

''I don't have to tell you what a proud man your
father was. I'm not totally surprised he didn't tell you
about the trouble with the farm.'' He poured the
strong black brew into their mugs and then reclaimed
his seat. ''He didn't tell me, either, for what it's
worth. I found out by accident.''

It was silly for her to be relieved. Childish, really.
She should have been glad her dad had such a good
friend, a person with whom to share stories and pass
the time. But she was comforted, too, that her father
hadn't chosen to confide in someone other than herself.

She shook her head. Childish *and* selfish.

''I know what you're thinking, and you've got to

stop beating yourself up.'' The sternness in his voice brought her thoughts up short.

''You have no idea what I'm thinking or feeling.''

''Guilt. Relief. Uncertainty. Numbness.'' He took a sip of coffee. ''Anger.''

''All a natural part of the grieving process. So, you got an A in psychology.'' She looked at her hands. She hadn't meant to sound so harsh, but he was right. She felt all those things and more.

''I know, because I experienced all those emotions when my wife died.''

Her gaze came up to meet his. ''I'm sorry. I had forgotten about—Dad told me what happened. I'm really sorry.''

''Thanks.'' He lifted a shoulder. ''It's been eight years.''

Her loss hit her full force, and she whispered, ''Does it get better?''

He reached across the table. ''Easier,'' he said quietly, covering her hand with his large one. ''Not better, just easier.''

Jenny focused on the way his hand totally devoured hers. Her fingers barely peeked out from his grasp. He could have lied with the intention of comforting her, but he hadn't—he'd told her like it was. Not better. Just easier. Someday she would surely appreciate his honesty. Right now she was too numb.

He squeezed her hand. ''You'll have reactions you would never have imagined, distraction will likely be a problem, but most of the time you'll be fine, and then a wave of sadness will unexpectedly knock you off your feet. But you'll pick yourself up and move on. Just do it at your own pace. No one can tell you how to grieve.''

''Thanks, Dr. McAlester. I, uh—'' She cleared her throat and withdrew her hand.

''Dr. McAlester?''

She looked into his amused eyes.

''No one calls me Dr. McAlester. Well, some of the older folks still refer to me as Doc. Call me Alex.''

''Okay. I've just always called you—'' She shrugged, wondering how old he was. Probably close to forty by now.

''You were a kid then.''

She sighed. ''Sometimes I wish I still were a kid.''

He smiled. ''Everyone does.''

''Even you?''

''Especially me.'' He winked and picked up the carafe. ''More coffee?''

His remark brought a smile to her lips—the first one since she'd received that horrible phone call. Her father. Dead of a heart attack. No warning.

Oh, God, how could this happen?

''Hey.'' Alex refilled her cup even though she'd barely touched it, and then his. ''We have to get practical. I hope you aren't planning on staying here.''

She cast a glance around the kitchen. It wasn't in too bad shape. ''I was…''

''Not a good idea.''

''Why?

''Besides the obvious?''

She stiffened at his frankness. "My father lived here. It was good enough for him."

"These old houses eventually require work. Not just for cosmetic reasons, but to keep them safe. Your father didn't have the resources, and the house really started to fall apart this past year or so. But he knew where the physical pitfalls were and he avoided them."

The truth made her shudder. She didn't want to hear this. None of it. She knew Alex was trying to help, but the guilt was already too strong.

"But I'm more concerned with you facing old memories." His voice was kind, gentle. "Tomorrow's the funeral. You don't want to be an emotional wreck by then."

She took a deep breath, hoping to suppress the hysterical laugh bubbling inside her chest. Emotional wreck? Her? Been there, done that.

"So I was thinking," he continued. "Maybe you ought to stay at my place. I have two extra rooms, and you'd have your own bathroom. Then we could go to the funeral together. Make sense?"

She hesitated, though it made more sense than he knew. Staying with him would save her the cost of a room at Twin Oaks Bed and Breakfast. And saving as much as a dollar was no small blessing these days.

But as she stared into his kind gray eyes, some crazy instinct told her to run the other way. "Thanks, but I'll be staying at the bed-and-breakfast."

CHAPTER TWO

NUMB AND SHAKING, Jenny watched as they lowered her father's casket into the ground. The wad of tissues she clutched in her hand had shredded some time ago. She should have accepted Maureen Cooper's linen handkerchief before they'd left the bed-and-breakfast.

But of course Jenny was too much like her father. Proud and headstrong and determined to handle everything on her own. Like him, she didn't need anyone's help, and now she was burying him. And her life was so screwed up she didn't know which way to turn.

God, she'd cried so much last night she thought for sure there'd be no more tears left. But they burned her eyes and slid uncontrollably down her cheeks. Her head had grown so light she prayed she wouldn't pass out.

"Here." Maureen pushed a folded square of linen into Jenny's hand.

Another of her dad's friends, Maureen had encouraged Jenny to drink a cup of tea and eat a piece of toast earlier this morning. Right now Jenny wasn't sure that had been such a good idea. Her stomach was coiled in knots, and she struggled to keep the nausea at bay.

Maureen had driven her to the funeral service at the Church of the Good Shepherd and then on to the cemetery. Alex had offered to pick her up, but she had declined. He was being nice, and she appreciated his concern, but something about him unsettled her.

Maybe it was because he knew her father so well. Alex had been Ed Taylor's closest friend since Jenny had left Cooper's Corner. If her father had felt deserted, Alex would know. And he would blame her.

She stared at the casket, her knees growing increasingly weak, until Maureen nudged her.

"The rose," she whispered.

Jenny looked blankly at her.

"They're waiting for you to throw in the rose."

Jenny looked at her hand. She'd forgotten she held the single yellow bloom. It seemed glued to her palm. She didn't want to throw it on top of the casket. She wanted someone to wake her, tell her she'd been having a nightmare.

God, this was so final. No more denial. No more thinking she'd go home and see her dad sitting on his recliner. She tried to pry her fingers from the stem, but she couldn't seem to manage it.

People began to murmur softly. She wouldn't look up to see the censure mixed with pity in their eyes. Let them think what they wanted.

"Jenny?"

She heard Alex's voice close to her ear, felt his hand at her elbow.

"Jenny, let me help you." He took her hand and unwrapped her fingers from around the rose.

She'd bent the stem halfway down so the bloom hung. But what did it matter? In seconds it would be covered with dirt. Just like her father.

A sob caught in her throat, and she tossed the rose on top of the polished cherry wood. Alex slipped an arm around her shoulders and held her against him as two men shoveled dirt on the casket.

She wanted to turn her face into his chest and wipe away the image of her father being buried. But she forced her gaze to remain on the workers and concentrated on taking deep even breaths.

"Come on, Jenny." A few minutes later Alex tried to steer her away from the gravesite, and when she demurred, he whispered, "Everyone is waiting to offer their condolences."

Oh, God. The sea of faces seem to blur together. Why didn't they all just go away? Leave her to mourn alone, in peace.

"I know you want them to disappear," Alex said quietly so that only she could hear. "But they're mourning him, too. Come on, it won't take long."

Ashamed that he'd read her selfish thoughts, she gazed at him. But she found no condemnation or disapproval. Only understanding. He had gone through this, too. He knew how she felt. It was both comforting and disturbing as she let him walk her toward the clusters of mourners, dabbing at their red eyes and even redder noses.

Two vanloads of flowers had been delivered earlier. Scarlet roses. Pink and white carnations. Lilies, spider mums. The arrangements were everywhere, their fragrances blending to fuel her queasiness.

"Isn't it odd?" She hadn't realized she'd murmured out loud until Alex dipped his head.

"What was that?"

"The custom of sending flowers to a funeral. They're so cheerful, and this is such a somber occasion."

Alex smiled and squeezed her shoulders. "Ready?"

She looked again at the expectant faces. They were so close. So stifling. The air seemed to grow thicker. She nodded.

"I'm so sorry, honey." Phyllis Cooper was the first to step up and clasp Jenny's cold hands in hers. "Your father is going to be sorely missed. He was a good man. Always the first one to offer a helping hand in times of trouble." She smiled fondly at Alex. "He and the doc here."

Her husband, Philo, urged her to move on. Behind him, a line had formed. Most of the people had known her father for fifty years. Alex was right. This was difficult for them, too.

"Thank you," Jenny said, forcing a smile. "For coming. For being his friend." Her voice broke, and Phyllis started to cry again as she was ushered away by Philo.

Clint Cooper, Maureen's brother, stepped up. "There aren't any words that will make it better, Jenny." He squeezed her hands. "If there's anything I can do…"

She nodded and gave him a faint smile. He was right. There were no words. But his warm hands were comforting, just like Alex's strong arm around her shoulders. She swayed slightly toward him, glad he was there to absorb her unsteady weight.

An older couple came after Clint. She didn't recognize them. They'd moved to Cooper's Corner five years ago, they explained, and often bought chickens from her father. She heard only half of what they said but just kept smiling. The scent of carnations and roses got stronger. More sickly.

She used the handkerchief to wipe the dampness coating the back of her neck. How many more people were there?

Alex tightened his hold on Jenny's slim shoulders. She didn't look well. Too pale and unsteady. The dark circles under her eyes had been there yesterday and were certainly understandable. But she was thin. Too thin. As if she'd been ill for a while.

"You're doing great," he whispered to her, and she sank heavily against him.

Maureen came to his other side. "I've got bottled water in the car. She looks as if she could use it."

He nodded. "I'd offer to go get it but—"

"No, she needs you to stay here." Maureen cast a concerned glance at Jenny before heading toward the parking lot.

"It's almost over," he said quietly.

Jenny shuddered.

At least half a dozen people still waited to offer their condolences. He knew it was important to them to do so, but damn, he wished he could get Jenny out of the sun and sitting down. That she hadn't once protested his self-appointed role as her guardian told him she wasn't herself.

Yesterday it seemed she couldn't get away from him fast enough. He didn't know what that was about, but he never questioned anything that had to do with the grieving process. When Sara died, he thought he'd go crazy. Everything that had been important to him crumpled to insignificance.

He couldn't eat, couldn't sleep. Even going to the clinic became a chore. If he hadn't been the only vet in town at the time, he probably would have hibernated for a year. He never wanted to go through that again. Never.

Maureen brought the water and handed it to him instead of to Jenny. Several people had given him speculative looks, probably because he'd practically stayed glued to Jenny. Most of them knew his close relationship with Ed, but there would of course be gossip. Unavoidable in a town this size. But if they didn't understand his desire to comfort the man's daughter, then tough.

"Jenny?"

She looked at him, her light brown eyes huge, haunted, her face still very pale.

"Here, have some water."

She moistened her lips. "I don't think I can."

"Just a little?"

"Okay."

He uncapped the bottle and handed it to her. But

something told him not to let go altogether as she tipped the bottle to her lips. She took a small sip. As he watched her throat work, noticed the moisture glistening on her lips, a totally inappropriate thought startled him.

Disgusted him.

He lowered the bottle and pulled away.

Her eyes widened. Surprised. Disoriented. And then they drifted closed as she crumpled to the ground.

ALEX SAT in the hospital waiting area, nervous as all get out. The sterile odor got to him, and he had to take frequent trips outside for fresh air. He hadn't been here since Sara died.

He checked his watch. Two hours. And all the doctor could tell him was that Jenny was sick. No kidding. That much he knew.

Was this what the owners of the pets he treated went through? Never again would he wait one minute longer than necessary to advise an owner of a diagnosis. Not that he ever made anyone wait, but he'd be a lot more conscious of time.

He loosened the tie he was unaccustomed to wearing. He only had two, one blue and one green. That's all he needed. He wore them to weddings and funerals.

Settling back in the chair, he rested his head against the wall and closed his eyes. Ed Taylor was really dead. Unbelievable. Yeah, the guy had fallen on some tough times, but he was still in perfect health. Alex knew he ate well because they shared dinner most nights. He'd been careful not to let Ed think it was charity.

It was easy to convince him that Alex was lonely and wanted the company. Ed was lonely, too. He missed Jenny. He talked about her all the time. Counted down the days when she'd promised to come home for a long weekend. Her visits had been too infrequent, especially over the past couple of years.

But that was none of Alex's business. What was important was getting her well. Maureen Cooper thought he'd overreacted by bringing Jenny to the hospital. A fainting spell wasn't serious, especially considering the circumstances, but he had this bad feeling....

"Alex?"

He set aside the stale coffee he'd been drinking and stood to shake Dr. Werner's hand. "Marvin, it's been a while."

"Too long. How have you been?"

Alex shrugged. "Hanging in there."

"You're here for the Taylor woman?"

Alex drew his head back in surprise. Dr. Werner operated in this hospital, so it wasn't unusual that he'd run into Sara's doctor. But how did he know about Jenny? "I'm waiting for her. Why?"

"How well do you know her?"

A sickening feeling came over Alex. "What's going on?"

The older man's expression looked grim. "Why don't we go to my office?"

"Were you on call? Why are you involved? She only fainted."

"Please, Alex." The doctor's weathered face creased in a sympathetic frown. "It would be better to go to my office."

Alex muttered a curse. He started to sweat. "Sure. Okay."

He shrugged out of his suit jacket and hooked it on his finger as he silently walked beside Marvin down the hall. He'd traveled this same path nine years ago, when he'd found out about the cancer growing inside Sara.

God, this couldn't be happening again.

Sara had been only thirty, as well.

Damn it. He was jumping the gun. Panicking for nothing. This was probably about Jenny's health insurance. Or maybe they wanted to keep her overnight for observation. Yeah, that was it.

"Have a seat, Alex." The doctor motioned to the overstuffed black leather chair facing his desk, then closed the door.

His office hadn't changed, except the walls seemed to be a little closer now. Alex tugged at the collar of his shirt. "Tell me what's going on," he said before the man could sit.

"Are you related to her?"

Alex shook his head. "She's here for her father's funeral. As far as I know, she doesn't have any other relatives."

The doctor pursed his lips in indecision.

"Don't do this to me, Marvin."

The man's expression softened. "Ethically I shouldn't be discussing her medical problems with you."

"I understand." He wouldn't accept anything less than a full explanation.

"But since she still isn't very coherent and we really need to keep her here…" He sighed. "It looks like she might have a tumor growing at the base of her spine."

"What?" Ed hadn't said a word to Alex. "Would she know about it?"

"I can't see how she wouldn't. She has to be in pain at times, maybe even have some difficulty walking and sitting. It's fairly large. It should have been removed by now." Marvin pinched the bridge of his nose. "Although it's in a tricky area."

Thoughts were spinning and colliding inside Alex's head. He couldn't think straight. "Are you sure? How did you discover it?"

"The ER doctor had X rays taken. He thought he felt something when he examined her. When she remained unresponsive, he went ahead with a couple of tests and the X rays."

"Good thing." Alex stared out the window, trying to gather his wits. "What now?"

Marvin stayed silent for so long, Alex looked at him. The man's face was a mask of concern. "You're assuming she didn't know about the tumor. I'm guessing she knows, but she's chosen not to do anything about it."

"That's crazy."

"Like I said, it's in a tricky area."

"Meaning?"

"It may not be worth the risk."

Alex took a deep breath. "Paralysis?"

"That's certainly possible."

"And?"

Marvin's somber gaze gave Alex the answer before he said, "If it's malignant, the prognosis would not be good."

The room spun. A cold sweat broke out down Alex's back. This wasn't a surprise, so why did he feel like the wind had been knocked out of him? "But she must know the tumor's benign, right? Or else she'd have surgery."

"Only she can answer that."

Alex wanted to punch a wall. "Anything else?"

"Are you okay?"

"Yeah."

"You don't look it."

"Of course I'm concerned," Alex said, "but I don't even know her that well."

"I suspect this has brought up some painful memories."

Alex shrugged. Hell, yeah, it brought up painful memories. But what was he supposed to do? Abandon Jenny? She was Ed's daughter. "Can I go see her?"

"She's in ICU. I'll take you in."

Both men stood. "Intensive care? Something you aren't telling me?"

"No, we'll be moving her shortly." Marvin paused at the door. "I advised you of her condition as a per-

sonal courtesy. It's strictly between us. You're going
to have to let her explain as if you have no knowledge
of her condition.''

"I understand, and I appreciate the confidence.''
Alex shook Marvin's hand again and followed him
out of the office. He knew it wasn't easy for an up-
standing doctor like Werner to breach a patient's con-
fidentiality. He'd relied on and trusted the information
Alex had given him about Jenny's lack of relatives.

The thing was, as far as Alex knew, Jenny really
was alone. Ed had never mentioned any serious boy-
friends. Of course, she might have chosen to keep that
aspect of her life from him. Just like she'd withheld
the information about her health.

This wasn't going to be easy—getting her to open
up to him. But Alex had to try. If she dug her heels
in and refused to discuss it, he'd be forced to back
off. Man, he hoped she wouldn't do that. Yet he
meant nothing to her, and if she hadn't told her own
father...

They stopped at the nurses' station, where the doctor gave orders to allow Alex free visitation. Two
doors down, Marvin motioned him inside. Jenny lay
on a bed, her eyes closed.

The doctor clapped him on the back, nodded and
then continued down the hall.

Alex stood frozen in the doorway. Jenny wasn't
hooked up to anything, not the way Sara had been
toward the end. But God, he hated hospitals. The
smells, the sounds, even the pale green walls. Pretty

sad for a vet who had to perform surgery at least twice a month. But that was different.

He stepped inside, his eyes trained on Jenny, waiting for some movement. For a moment he thought he saw her lashes flutter, but it was a trick of the lighting and his own tired eyes.

Had they given her medication for pain? She hadn't complained of any at the cemetery, but he doubted she would have. He turned to ask the nurse at the station. They had to have given her something. She shouldn't still be out like this.

"Alex?"

He swung around. Jenny was trying to sit up. "Hey, easy does it."

She blinked and sank down under the encouraging pressure of his hand. "What happened?"

"You fainted."

She frowned and put a hand to her head. "Oh, my God. We were at the cemetery. All those people..."

"Relax," he said, keeping his hand on her shoulder when she tried to sit up again. "You're not the first person to faint at a funeral service."

Her gaze surveyed the room. "I'm in a hospital?"

"Yes. Community General."

"For fainting?"

"I couldn't get you to come to. I thought it best—"

She jerked away from him and tried to sit up again. "I can't be here."

He couldn't keep restraining her, and she sat upright. "Why not?"

"Where are my clothes?" She clutched the front of the gown once she realized all she had on was the thin cotton hospital issue.

"Probably in the closet. The doctor hasn't released you yet."

"I don't care." She moved to the edge of the bed. The back of the gown opened, exposing her pale slim back. She twisted around, trying to cover herself. "Would you mind looking in the closet for me?"

"Yes."

She blinked. "Excuse me?"

"You haven't been released from the doctor's care yet."

"For Pete's sake, I only fainted. You said yourself I'm not the first to pass out at a funeral."

Alex forced himself to stay calm. He realized from the panicked look on her face that she knew about the tumor, but she wasn't going to tell him. And he wasn't about to let her leave here. "They took X rays."

"What?" The panic slid into anger. "Who gave them the right?"

"The doctor thought he felt something at the base of your spine."

"That's ridiculous." She quickly averted her gaze, but then anger brought her attention to him. "They told you that?"

"I overheard."

"Damn it." She exhaled loudly.

"Why are you so edgy?" He kept his voice low and soothing, hoping to lessen her agitation.

"Because I don't have medical insurance, that's why. And this all has to cost a fortune."

The information threw him. "Aren't you covered by your job?"

She looked away again. "No. I really wish you'd get my clothes."

Alex knew what hotel chain she worked for—a large international company. They would offer insurance. Legally, they *had* to offer it. Unless she no longer worked for them and hadn't told Ed.

"Fine. I'll get them myself." She hopped off the bed, trying to keep the hospital gown from gaping.

"Okay." He went to the closet and found her navy blue suit. He had no intention of dropping the subject, but he knew he wouldn't get anywhere now.

She stared at him, her clothes clutched to her chest. "Would you please wait outside?"

"Oh, yeah, of course." His thoughts had been speeding like a runaway train.

While she changed, he told the duty nurse Jenny would be leaving, then he left a note for Dr. Werner to call him. What he wanted to tell the man he had no idea. But they had to do something.

Jenny opened the door. Her complexion was devoid of color, and she looked frailer than she had this morning. The smile she gave him didn't reach her eyes. "How about giving me a ride to the B and B?"

He shook his head. "You're coming home with me."

CHAPTER THREE

ALEX POURED them each some peppermint tea and set the cups on the table. Jenny had remained stubbornly silent the entire way to his house. Too bad. She was here and she was going to talk to him.

"Do you want sugar or lemon or anything with that?"

Arms folded across her chest, she shook her head. "Technically, I believe you've kidnapped me."

He indicated the phone with a jut of his chin. "The number to the police department is written inside the phone book."

Her lips twitched. "Very funny."

He took a seat at the table. "I should remind you that I did not force you into my car."

"Yeah, but—" She sighed. "Okay, what do you want?"

"The truth."

She eyed him for a moment. "What gives you the right to ask about my business?"

"It's not about having the right. I was your father's friend. He's not here, and I'd like to think I'm acting on his behalf."

Pain narrowed her eyes. "That's not fair."

He scrubbed at his face and sank back in the chair. It probably wasn't fair to bring up Ed, but Alex was desperate. He also meant what he'd said. He owed Ed a stab at trying to help Jenny.

"Look," she said, her voice softening. "I know you mean well, but this isn't your problem."

"I know, but I can still want to help."

Her light brown eyes got a little glassy, and she sniffed. "You can't."

"Let me be the judge of that."

"There's too much you don't understand."

He hesitated, hoping he wasn't about to open a can of worms. Damn it. He had to tell her. Reaching for her hand, he said, "I know about the tumor."

She jerked away from him. He heard her sharp intake of breath. "I don't know what you're talking about."

"Yes, you do. How long, Jenny?"

She shot up from the table and picked up the phone.

"What are you doing?" He went to her and took the receiver out of her hand. Her skin was ice cold.

"Please give that back to me so I can call a cab."

"You don't need to do that."

"Will you take me to the B and B? Now?"

"After we talk."

She moved aside, but he caught her by her shoulders. She was so slight she felt like a child.

"Alex, please don't do this." Her eyes were glistening and pleading, and he almost gave in.

"What would be the harm in talking to me?" he

asked in a low, soothing voice. "Whatever you say stays right here. Between us."

She sighed heavily, and he could almost feel the fight drain from her. "You're right about the tumor. How did you know?"

"I saw the X rays."

Anger sparked in her eyes. "The doctor showed them to you?"

He shook his head, hating that he lied, but he had to protect Marvin. "I saw the radiologist studying them. I'm a vet. I look at X rays all the time. Animals and people aren't that different."

She looked skeptical. "Pretty sloppy hospital if they let everyone nose around."

He smiled. "Can we sit down and finish our tea?"

She nodded, and he found he was reluctant to release her. So small and fragile, she stirred a protective instinct in him that had long ago gone dormant.

Jenny moved first, and he lowered his hands. She seemed grateful to be sitting again, and lifted the cup to her lips. "Let me heat that tea up."

"It's fine. Really."

He sat down, thinking what he needed right now was a shot of whiskey. Strong. Straight up. "Can I get you anything else? Some toast or crackers maybe?"

"No, thanks."

"You should try to eat something."

"Trust me. I can't."

He didn't push. Just then, a scratching sounded at

the door. "Aw, shoot. I forgot about Bagel." He got up and let the golden retriever in.

Jenny gasped.

Alex grabbed Bagel's collar before he made a bee-line to her. "Sorry, I should have asked if you were okay with dogs."

"Of course I am." She held out the back of her hand for Bagel to sniff, and Alex let him go. "He's beautiful."

"Not too loud. He already has a swelled head."

She laughed and scratched the dog's ears. He was putty in her hands. "You're so pretty, aren't you?"

"He'll be three next month and still thinks he's a puppy."

"That's okay. Nobody wants to grow up, do they, boy?" She stroked his back, then ruffled the fur near his jaw just the way he liked.

This was a new side to Jenny, Alex thought. Even her face had relaxed, and she looked young and care-free. Just as she should.

But it wouldn't last. They still had to talk.

"Come on, Bagel, let's get you some chow." He drew the dog's attention by getting a can of food out of the cupboard. "I'll only be a minute."

"Take your time."

He smiled at the glint of mischief in her eyes. "Don't worry, I'll be back before you know it."

"Great."

That he glimpsed some humor gave him hope, and he hurried to feed Bagel. When he returned less than a minute later, Jenny was pouring them both more tea.

"Thanks." He reclaimed his seat and waited for her to begin.

She took a couple of unhurried sips, her brows furrowed in thought. She was probably trying to edit what she was about to say. Setting the cup down, she sighed. "My doctor discovered the tumor about six months ago."

"You've known a long time."

"Longer than that…I mean, I didn't know it was a tumor, but I've been sick for almost two years."

Alex shook his head. "What took them so long to diagnose you?"

"Because of where the tumor is located, my symptoms mimicked several other diseases. They kept running tests that came out negative."

"For a year and a half?"

She made a wry face. "I didn't exactly go to the doctor right away. I'd broken my leg and hurt my back skiing the year before, and I thought that was where the pain had come from. But it wasn't just pain. I'd get really weak and my legs felt as if they couldn't hold me up. Kind of like when you have a bad case of the flu."

"So you put off going to the doctor."

She shrugged. "I was busy at work with the new hotel opening." Her laugh held no humor. "The irony is that when I couldn't keep up the pace, I got fired."

"Why didn't you go on medical disability?"

"I hadn't been diagnosed yet."

"But you knew something was wrong."

Jenny shook her head. "I thought it was fatigue, that my boss was right and I simply wasn't up to the task of opening a new hotel. So when they gave me the opportunity to resign rather than have my records show I was fired, I accepted." Admirably, she didn't look bitter when she added, "But there was no mistaking the fact I was fired."

"Legally your health insurance didn't have to stop."

"I kept the coverage and paid for it myself. But it was difficult to find another job when I couldn't even get out of bed some days. I've been living off my savings. I lost my insurance the month before they found the tumor."

Alex didn't know what to say. So many things made sense now. "So basically, money is the only thing holding you back from having surgery."

She put her cup down and stared at it. "It's more complicated than that. The tumor is encased in nerves, which makes the surgery risky. Only a few doctors can perform the operation."

"And you haven't found one to take your case?"

"Not exactly." Her lips curved in a wry smile. "I haven't found one to do it for free. The cost will be incredibly high, plus there'd be months of physical therapy."

Alex let the information sink in. He had money put away, but he doubted it was enough to cover everything she was talking about. "Your dad didn't know any of this."

"Oh, God, no. He couldn't have done anything but worry."

"At least you would have had a place to stay."

"I'm an optimist. The specialist I need practices in New York." She laughed humorlessly. "I guess I was hoping for a miracle."

Alex was at a total loss. He had no answers. No advice. No nothing. "What are you going to do?"

She lifted a shoulder. She looked so frail, so resigned. "The same thing I've been doing. Work the odd temp job on days I feel well enough. Sometimes doctors will do a freebie now and again."

He wanted to ask what would happen if she didn't have the surgery, but he couldn't do it. "How about some dinner?"

She smiled. "Not hungry. How about you take me back to the B and B?"

"Maybe you should stay here."

"I'm heading back to New York tomorrow."

"Why so soon? Don't you want to go through some of your dad's things?"

Her eyes welled up. "I can't. Not yet."

How stupid of him. Of course it was too soon. He knew better. "Yeah, I understand."

She got up from the table. "I can still call a cab."

"No way." He pushed his chair back. "I'll take you. Maybe I can still talk you into having dinner with me along the way."

She smiled. "Thanks anyway, Doc."

He watched her walk out the back door ahead of

him. She looked so small and defeated. And damn, but he didn't have a clue how to help her.

"SIT AND HAVE some coffee with me." Maureen Cooper motioned to a chair. "I heard the shower. Jenny should be down shortly."

Alex accepted the steaming mug from Maureen. "How's she doing?"

Maureen joined him at the table. "I didn't see much of her last night. After you dropped her off, she chatted a few minutes with the twins and me and then went to her room."

"She didn't eat any dinner?"

"None that I know of. She refused my offer of meat loaf and mashed potatoes. What did the doctor say yesterday?"

Alex cradled the warm mug in his hands and stared thoughtfully at the dark brew. He had to be careful what he said about Jenny. Not just because it wasn't right to discuss her personal problems, but also because he thought he might have a solution for her. One that would require the utmost discretion regarding her medical condition.

"I didn't really talk to him. I assumed it wasn't anything serious, probably stress and fatigue."

"I bet she's pretty shocked." Maureen glanced over her shoulder toward the doorway. "Ed never had a history of heart disease and he seemed fine when I saw him just a few days before he died."

"Unfortunately, that's not unusual."

"I guess." Maureen seemed distracted. "The medical examiner still maintains Ed died of natural causes.''

Alex frowned. ''Why wouldn't he?''

Her eyes met his, uncertainty clear in their green depths. ''No reason. It's just that—well, don't you think it's odd that with no serious health problems or history of heart disease, he suddenly has a fatal heart attack?''

Alex glanced toward the doorway. This was a conversation Jenny didn't need to hear. ''I wouldn't say it's odd, certainly not unheard of. People die without warning from heart attacks all the time.''

Her somber gaze fastened on his. ''Did I tell you I found him with the box of chocolates I'd given him? He'd already had a couple of pieces.''

Alex was at a loss to make the connection. ''I'm not following you.''

She hesitated. ''A guest had left the chocolates with a thank-you note. I don't like the twins having so much sugar so I gave the box to Ed.''

Ed wasn't diabetic. ''What does that have to do with Ed's death?''

She frowned, her gaze wandering toward the window. And then she looked at him and smiled. ''Nothing. I'm being silly.''

He shot a quick glance toward the door, wary of Jenny overhearing and getting upset. ''Finding a dead body is traumatic enough. Finding a friend is horrifying. You have every right to be disconcerted.''

''We should hear Jenny—the bottom stair usually

creaks," Maureen assured him, lowering her voice. "Anyway, you're right. Let's forget it."

Troubled eyes belied her words. "Maureen, listen, what you're doing is quite common." People did it with their pets all the time. "You were the one who found him. It was a shock. There's no rhyme or reason to his death, but you're searching anyway. Ed died of natural causes. There is no blame here. The medical examiner would have determined otherwise during the autopsy."

Maureen forced a smile. "You're right." She'd been foolish to bring up the subject, she decided, except she wasn't thinking straight. Responsibility for Ed's death nagged at her.

She suspected Owen Nevil was involved. The man was ruthless. He hated her guts for having gathered enough evidence to get his brother, Carl, convicted of murder in New York. He could have left the poisoned chocolates for her, and he wouldn't stop at this failed attempt.

Most people didn't realize there were poisons that didn't show up on toxicology screens. No reason people should. No reason for them to know about her life as a cop in New York, either. But she'd done all she could for now. She'd taken steps to have the chocolates analyzed. She trusted Scott Hunter. He'd taken the chocolates to the forensic lab for her. So far, nothing had been found.

Alex watched Maureen briefly close her troubled eyes. He'd had no idea how hard it had been on her, finding Ed. "Nothing that happened is your fault. You were unlucky enough to be the one to find Ed. That's all." When she wouldn't look up, he tugged at her hand. "Understand?"

"Yeah, I understand."

"Could you try to sound a little more convincing?"

She smiled. "Yeah, yeah." And then her expression sobered. "Just be careful, okay?"

He frowned. "Is there something more you aren't telling me?"

She reached over and covered one of his hands with hers. "No. You're a good man, Alex. Thanks for listening to my crazy ramblings."

The step creaked, and they both looked toward the door. It must have been a floorboard, because Jenny was already standing there, her gaze trained on the hand Maureen had laid over Alex's.

Maureen quickly withdrew it. "Good morning."

"Hi." Jenny's gaze went to Alex. "I didn't know you'd be here."

"Have a seat." Maureen got up. "I'll get you some coffee. The other guests have eaten, but I'll fix you some strawberries and cantaloupe and freshly baked blueberry muffins."

"Just coffee will be fine."

"Wrong." Alex rose from the table and went over to the counter to retrieve the bowl of fruit.

"Excuse me?" Her hair was still a little damp, she wore no makeup, and the freckles stood out across her nose, making her look really young.

"You have to eat, Jenny."

Her gaze skittered to Maureen, who busied herself with the coffee.

"I'm going to be leaving soon," Jenny said, her voice tight with annoyance. "I'll pick something up while I'm on the road."

"I need to talk to you," he insisted.

Her gaze flew to Maureen again.

He took Jenny by the elbow. "Let's go sit in the living room. Okay with you, Maureen?"

"Be my guest." She didn't even look up.

"Wait a minute—" Jenny tried to put the brakes on.

"Would you rather we talk in here?" He sent a meaningful look toward Maureen.

Jenny glared at him, then led the way into the large gathering room. She didn't sit on the sofa but stood with her arms folded. "It's not that I don't appreciate you taking me to the hospital yesterday and waiting for me and all that, but you can't ride roughshod over me. I won't let you."

Alex wondered how much of his conversation she'd overheard. He didn't want Maureen's suspicions hanging over Jenny's head—she had enough on her plate.

"Did you know Maureen found your father?" he asked, testing the waters.

"Maureen?" Her eyes widened in genuine surprise and her gaze drifted toward the kitchen. "Oh, my God, she didn't tell me."

"It's not that important. I just wondered if you knew. She was good to him, inviting him for holiday dinners and stocking him up with food whenever he delivered his free-range chickens to her. She was actually picking up her order at Ed's place when she found him.''

"I had no idea. Thank you for telling me." She started to return to the kitchen.

"Wait," he said, satisfied she hadn't overheard anything upsetting. "That's not what I wanted to talk to you about."

Alarm flashed in her eyes again.

"Why don't we sit?"

She shook her head. "I'll be sitting the entire ride back to New York."

"Okay." He paused, knowing she wasn't going to make this easy. "I think I have a solution to your problem."

Interest sparked in her eyes. But then she drew back subtly with a wary expression. "I didn't ask for your help."

Alex had expected her to balk. Father and daughter were as stubborn as they came. "Will you at least listen, or are you going to let pride stand in the way of your health?"

Her expression turned sheepish. "Okay. I'll listen."

Alex cleared his throat. He really wished they were sitting down. "Marry me."

CHAPTER FOUR

JENNY STARED at Alex. She thought he had just asked her to marry him. She was losing it for sure. Maybe it wasn't a good idea to drive to New York today. One day of rest would be more prudent.

"Jenny?"

"Maybe I do need to sit down."

He put a hand on her lower back, guiding her to the sofa, and sat beside her. "I guess I should explain my line of thinking."

"That would help." Not that she was certain she wanted to hear this.

"I gave it a lot of thought last night. I have savings and investments but probably not enough to cover—"

She gasped. "Of course not. I wouldn't accept your money. I didn't tell you about the surgery so you'd—"

"Jenny, please." He held up a hand. "I know that. Let me finish."

Difficult as it was, she kept her mouth shut, but her thoughts went haywire. Alex didn't owe her anything. Why was he doing this?

"You can't get insurance, not with having already

been diagnosed. But if we were to get married, you would automatically be covered under my policy."

She stared at him, dumbfounded. "You can't be serious."

"Why not? It makes sense." His face darkened suddenly. "The marriage would be in name only."

"I know." She hadn't even thought that far yet. What he was proposing was crazy.

"You'd have to live at my place for appearances. We don't need the insurance company getting suspicious, and if they nose around, we'll be covered. But you'd have your own room, your own space. No one but us need know the circumstances of the marriage."

He looked so calm, so in control, yet tired. As if he'd stayed awake most of the night figuring out the logistics and ramifications of his offer.

"I don't know." She could barely form a coherent sentence. "I have to think about it."

"What's there to think about? You have no money and no job."

She flinched.

"I'm not trying to be cruel. I simply want you to understand there is no room for pride or emotion here. This is your chance to get your life back."

Her palms had grown clammy, and she dragged them over her jeans. "This is risky. If the insurance company finds out, you'll be in legal trouble."

He lifted a brow. "Believe me, I've thought of that. I'm not in the habit of defrauding an insurance company. But we're talking about your health, Jenny. If you don't have the surgery…"

He didn't finish the sentence, but she knew what he was thinking. If it hadn't been for a year of intense therapy, she'd be doing nothing *but* think about the consequences of leaving the growing tumor.

"I did some research last night," he continued. "Your recovery time, with physical therapy, can take up to eight months. You'll stay with me until you're fully well again, and then you leave. Go back to New York, Boston. Wherever you want. You'll owe me nothing."

A lump had lodged in her throat, and she wasn't sure she could speak. Not that she knew what to say. This was an incredibly generous offer. He'd been a good friend to her father, but she scarcely knew Alex.

She cleared her throat, and after two attempts asked, "Why are you doing this?"

His mouth curved in a smile that warmed his eyes and turned them a remarkable shade of gray. "If you have to ask, you've lived in the city too long."

She gave a nervous laugh. "You have to admit, this is kind of over the top."

He shrugged. "There's nothing your father wouldn't have done for anyone in this community."

She nodded. That was the truth, but it didn't give her a free pass, especially since she'd fled as soon as she was able. "I want you to think about this some more," she said, and he started to protest, but she held up her hand. "This time let me talk."

"Okay." He relaxed against the sofa, his long legs stretched in front of him. His jeans were old and faded but neatly pressed.

"You said yourself we're talking about a long recovery period. Throw in the time we have to wait for the insurance to kick in and getting an appointment with the specialist, the preparation and surgery itself, and we might be looking at over a year."

He nodded patiently.

At his apparent indifference, annoyance nudged her. "That's a long time."

"Are you done?"

"I can't ask you to put your life on hold like that."

He spread his hands. "How would my life be on hold? I work at the clinic six days a week and then I come home each evening. Nothing would change. Of course I'd check on you while you're home recovering and make sure you'd get to physical therapy, but that's nothing."

"I meant your personal life."

He frowned. "I just described my life."

"What about a love interest?" Her gaze wandered toward the kitchen, and a thought suddenly occurred to her. Maybe that's what he and Maureen had been discussing when Jenny came downstairs. They'd looked awfully cozy, hands clasped, voices lowered…

Alex laughed. It was a nice sound, and she liked the way his eyes crinkled at the corners, as if he laughed a lot. "That's nothing to worry about, I assure you."

"Aren't you seeing anyone?"

"No." He followed her gaze toward the kitchen. "Not Maureen, if that's what you're thinking."

"No," she said quickly. "Okay, so I thought maybe there was something going on there."

"Nope. She's a nice lady, and I like her a lot. But she's only a friend."

Jenny experienced an odd kind of relief. Why, she had no clue. "But there may be someone else. Not right now. But later, in five or six months. You might even find someone you want to marry—"

The amusement left his face. "That won't happen," he said quietly.

"You say that now, but you don't know."

"I know. I've already been married. It was great. I loved Sara. I still do. But she's gone."

Jenny shuddered at the finality in his voice. Pain shadowed his eyes. She'd put it there by bringing up the subject. If only she'd kept her big mouth shut.

"Look, Jen, I've already thought long and hard about what this arrangement will mean. I didn't make the offer lightly. All you have to do is accept, and we'll get the ball rolling."

"Why did you call me Jen?"

His eyebrows dipped in a frown. "I didn't realize I had."

"I like it." She smiled. "It sounds more mature than Jenny but not as stuffy as Jennifer."

"Good. Then I'll try to remember to make it Jen." He held her gaze, no hesitation showing in his. "So, what do you say? Will you marry me?"

The way his full lips lifted in a slow smile shouldn't have caused a nervous flutter in her tummy. She swallowed hard. "Yes," she said, wishing she didn't sound so darn breathless. The proposal wasn't for real. "I'll marry you."

IF TOM CHRISTEN was surprised by the sudden request to officiate their marriage, he didn't show it. Alex had liked the Episcopal priest the moment he'd met him. Even though the marriage wasn't for real, Alex was glad Tom would perform the ceremony.

"Are you ready?" His friend and partner, Tuck McCabe, ducked his head into the room as Alex was fighting a losing battle with his tie.

"I can't believe I have to wear a suit for the second time in three days," Alex muttered.

Tuck grinned. "You could've just worn a sport coat and slacks."

"Yeah, I know." He'd decided against showing up at church dressed too casually. Even though Tuck knew the true reason for the marriage, Alex figured he ought to keep up the appearance that the ceremony was a very special occasion for him.

"Maureen called. She's on her way. I'll tell everyone you'll be out in five minutes, okay?"

Alex nodded and kept struggling with the tie. It wasn't as if he didn't know how to do the damn thing. What was his problem? Anyone would think he was *really* getting married today.

He hoped it was a good decision to exclude guests. Both he and Jen decided the quieter they kept things, the better. Let people get used to her being around town. Maybe then there wouldn't be so much gossip.

The important thing was to get the insurance paper-work in motion.

As far as Tuck knowing the truth, Alex needed a witness to stand up for him, and although Tuck was a relative newcomer to Cooper's Corner, he and Alex had hit it off right away. Their professional partner-ship gave Alex some freedom from work that he hadn't had before, and Tuck was a good listener when Alex needed him.

"Damn it." He fumbled the knot again.

"Alex?"

In the mirror, he saw Jen step tentatively into the room. It was a small space in the front of the church behind the altar, and she stayed near the door.

"Did you need some help?" She looked pretty in a yellow linen suit, her long hair pulled into some kind of twist. She looked scared, too. Probably be-cause she'd walked in to find him cursing...and in church, no less.

He sighed. "I don't know why I'm having so much trouble with this."

She looked at her hands briefly, then met his gaze. "You can still change your mind, you know. I wouldn't blame you at all."

He let go of the tie and turned to her. "I haven't changed my mind."

She crossed her arms and hugged herself. "But you can if you want."

"I'm not going to." He moved toward her and saw her stiffen, but that didn't stop him. He reached for her, grasping her shoulders and waiting for her to look into his eyes. "I'm not having second thoughts. I just hate messing with ties."

A startled laugh escaped her, easing the tension. "I can help."

"Yeah?"

She nodded and took hold of the slippery blue silk. "I used to wear ties to work all the time."

"Like these?"

"Yep."

"You're kidding." He lifted his chin to give her room, wishing he faced the mirror so he could watch her.

"Women can wear ties, too." She tugged the knot tight, her indignation evident.

He stretched his neck to loosen the silk noose. "Yeah, but why in the heck would you?"

She smiled. "There. What do you think?"

He turned toward the mirror. "Good job."

"I have my uses."

Their gazes met in the mirror. "Thanks."

She looked away first. "No problem. I'll be waiting outside. I mean, in the church. Just outside here." A pretty pink spread across her cheeks, and she promptly turned to leave.

What had suddenly gotten her so nervous? "Hey, Jen, wait."

With obvious reluctance, she faced him again.

He held out a hand to her, and she briefly looked as if she would ignore it, then slipped her hand in his. "Are you having second thoughts?"

She slowly shook her head.

"Is something wrong?"

Again she said nothing, but she shook her head.

"Would you tell me if there was?"

That earned him a faint smile. "Maybe," she replied honestly.

He tugged her toward him, and when she got close, she tipped her head to look at him with wide, uncertain eyes. "We're doing the right thing," he said.

"I hope so."

"No question about it." He kissed the tip of her nose.

She blinked, looking as if she wanted to say something. She didn't, though, and gave him a shy smile instead.

"What did you want to say?" he asked quietly.

She drew in her lower lip. She had perfectly straight white teeth, and an old image of her in braces flashed in his mind.

"Come on, out with it."

She closed her eyes. "I really need a hug."

That was the last thing he'd expected her to say. He smiled when she finally peeked out from under her lashes. "What a coincidence. So do I."

He slid his arms around her and held her close. Her hair smelled like peaches, and her soft sigh seemed to go right through the wall of his chest. She was so small and fragile he was afraid to squeeze too tight. To his amazement, he wanted to. He wanted to hold her so close that they melted together.

What the hell was the matter with him? This was

Jenny Taylor. Ed's daughter. This was about taking care of her, getting her well.

He started to retreat, but she hugged his waist and clung to him as if her life depended on it. And sadly, maybe it did. This was gratitude. Nothing else.

His body didn't get it. The last thing he wanted was for her to feel the tightening arousal that stunned him beyond comprehension. "We're late," he said as he drew back, hoping like hell nothing showed under his fly.

She nodded and gave him a shaky smile. "Thank you."

He reached for his suit jacket. "Oh, yeah, that was a real hardship."

The pleasure in her eyes warmed him. "I'll meet you out there."

He glanced at his watch. "We have two minutes."

"Alex?" She stopped at the door. "Thanks."

"Stop thanking me," he said gruffly, and she left with a smile.

As soon as the door closed, he let out a frustrated sigh. He felt relieved, disgusted and astonished, and his brain was spinning. So, he was a normal red-blooded male. If he didn't react to a pretty woman, he'd be worried. No need to beat up on himself.

But this was Jenny Taylor.

Damn.

He went to the small sink in the corner and splashed water on his face. At least she didn't seem to know about his perverted reaction. Nah, perverted was too strong. His body was only seeking something it hadn't had in a very long time. Too long.

Three years after Sara had died, he'd gone on a few dates. He'd really liked a vet from Boston he'd met at a conference. They'd dated for the longest period of time, almost a year. But when push came to shove, he knew the relationship couldn't go anywhere. He'd been honest with Janet about his feelings, and she'd been understandably upset. He hadn't seen her since then.

With Jenny, he was safe. The marriage was more like a business arrangement. No personal feelings were involved. Once she was well and on her feet, she'd head back to the big city. She'd never stick around a place like Cooper's Corner.

He dried his face and hands, feeling only marginally better. There was no ignoring the nagging unease that had plagued him since he'd opened his eyes this morning. Not that he had any reservations about what they were doing. That was the one point he was very clear about.

Maybe his edginess had to do with the whole church and wedding thing. Perhaps subconsciously it reminded him of Sara, though their wedding day had been nothing like today. They knew from their sophomore year in college that they'd eventually marry. Sara had planned the wedding ceremony and reception down to the last white orchid by the time he'd graduated from veterinarian school. They'd tied the knot a month later.

He smiled at the memory of how beautiful she'd

looked in the white wedding gown her mother and
grandmother had worn before her. Sara and he had
had so many youthful plans, so many dreams.

All of them cut short.

He took a deep breath and shook off the melancholy. No room for that kind of thinking today. Jen
would probably pick up the bad vibes, and she was
already fragile and uncertain. They needed to get
through the day in peace and privacy, file the insurance forms and then prepare for the reaction and com-
ments from everyone.

The news of their wedding had probably been
picked up already by Phyllis and Philo Cooper's ra-
dar, and it wouldn't take the couple long to spread
the word. They were the town's best source of gossip,
though their interest in people was genuine and not
the least bit malicious. They loved to be the first in
the know.

Alex took a last look at his reflection, adjusted his
white starched collar and stepped into the hall. The
church was quiet when he entered. Tom Christen,
Tuck and his wife Grace, and Jenny awaited him. He
and Jen had decided to skip an organist. No frills.
Fast and simple. That should provide all kinds of fodder for the local grapevine.

The assembled group was standing at the front of
the church, talking. He smiled at the thought that it
was usually the bride who was late, tending to last-
minute details.

Jenny looked at him and smiled back. She really
did look pretty. And tall. With the white heels she

wore, she had to be about five ten. Nice. He was six six, and to him, most women seemed short.

Maureen entered from the back of the church and hurried up the aisle. "Sorry I'm late," she murmured. "The twins decided to try their hand at plumbing."

Jenny grinned. "Thanks for coming."

Alex nodded his thanks to her. He and Jenny had decided Maureen was the logical choice to be Jen's witness. She was discreet and had been a friend of Ed's. Alex knew she wouldn't ask questions, even if she suspected there was more to the marriage than the traditional reason.

"Shall we get started?" Tom asked.

Alex and Jenny glanced at each other, and both nodded as they moved closer together. Impulsively he took her hand. It felt small and delicate, and he had an overwhelming desire to protect her from all of life's hardships.

She squeezed his hand as Tom began the service. At Alex's request, the priest kept the words brief, and within ten minutes they were pronounced husband and wife. Before Tom instructed him to kiss his bride, Alex pulled Jenny into his arms and gave her a hug. No one seemed to notice the missing kiss.

After he and Jenny signed the marriage certificate, he quickly shook Tom's hand, then ushered Jenny down the aisle. Tuck and Maureen stayed behind a moment to add their signatures.

"We haven't talked about what we should do this evening," he whispered before they got to the door.

She stopped and stared at him. "This evening?"

He nodded, confused by the wariness in her eyes. "You know, like going out to dinner or doing something special. Even if it's just for show."

"Oh." She frowned slightly. "Alone?"

"Well, I would ask Tuck, but I know he and his wife, Grace, have plans. We should ask Maureen in appreciation of standing in for us."

"She probably has to get back to Twin Oaks."

"Then I guess it's you and me." He shrugged. "But we don't have to do anything, either. Nobody knows about us yet. We can lay low for tonight. Enjoy the peace and quiet while we can."

"That gets my vote. I'm a little tired. Sorry."

"Hey, don't be sorry. Staying home and relaxing is fine by me. I've got your room ready. I'll move in whatever you have with you. We'll worry about getting the rest of your stuff later in the week."

She smiled with relief. "Thanks. I'm about ready to put my feet up."

Tuck, Grace and Maureen were on their way down the aisle to join them as Alex pushed open the mahogany door.

"Surprise!"

He put a protective hand up when raw rice pelted them. "What the hell!"

Phyllis and Philo Cooper, Howard and Gina Monroe and at least a dozen other well-wishers had been lying in wait.

CHAPTER FIVE

"Would you like more potato salad, dear?" Phyllis Cooper seemed to have made it her mission to fatten Jenny up. "Or how about some of this lovely Waldorf salad? Martha Dorn made it. Everyone wants the recipe, but she won't budge."

"No, thank you. Really. I'm beyond stuffed." Jenny put a hand to her stomach. And not just for effect, either. She truly did feel a little under the weather.

She appreciated the last-minute potluck everyone had scrambled to make possible. In fact, when she'd realized what all these kind people had done in honor of Alex and her wedding, she'd been reduced to tears. But that didn't alter the fact that if she ate one more piece of fried chicken or wedge of homemade chicken pot pie, she really would be sick.

"Hey." Alex sat beside her on Philo and Phyllis Cooper's couch. "How are you holding up?"

"I have never eaten so much food in my entire life or smiled so much in two hours. Other than that, I'm peachy. What about you?"

He didn't smile but narrowed his gaze. "You look flushed."

"I am a little warm."

"Come on." He got up and pulled her with him.

Everyone turned to see where they were going, approving smiles on their faces.

Jenny didn't ask where he was taking her. She smiled at everyone and followed Alex. Not that she had a choice. He wouldn't let go of her hand until they were outside on the Coopers' back porch.

She breathed in the cool spring air, sighing as she exhaled.

"Feel better?"

"Much." She leaned against a white post. "There's got to be three dozen people crammed in there."

"At least." He sat on the swing chair and patted the spot beside him.

She obliged, although it was a tight squeeze. "How did they find out?"

"Phyllis, of course, was the instigator. She overheard Grace—Tuck's wife—ordering flowers for the church."

Jenny chuckled, even though she was tired and anxious. "Phyllis Cooper hasn't changed a bit. When I was in high school, and some of the other kids tried to talk me into cutting class, I was more afraid of her finding out than my own father."

He smiled. "I can't imagine you cutting school."

"There's a lot about me you don't know, Dr. McAlester."

"Ah, sounds like a challenge."

"No, I'm too tired."

His expression grew serious. "It's been a long day for you. We'll make our exit soon. We're officially newlyweds—they can't expect us to hang around here."

"I'm okay, really. Just tired. It was incredibly nice of them to pull this together on such short notice."

"Yeah, but I still wish we'd had time to ourselves first. Make sure our stories meshed."

"No one has said much to me." Jenny looked through the window into the house. People stood shoulder to shoulder, laughing and talking and eating. "Now that dinner is over, they may start asking questions. Has anyone expressed their surprise to you?"

Alex followed her gaze. "Actually, I overheard Phyllis telling Trudi Karr from over at the diner that she knew about us all along just from the way I looked at you in town the other day. Leave it to Phyllis to want everyone to think she knows it all."

"When did you see me in town?"

"The day you arrived. Before I came out to the farm. You stopped to drop a piece of mail in a post-box."

"Where were you?"

"Up a tree." He made a wry face. "That's why I couldn't catch you in time. I was just climbing down with a kitten who'd gotten stuck up there."

"You're always rescuing people or animals." Jenny tilted her head to the side. "What do you do for you?"

Alex frowned, looking uncomfortable. "That's an odd question."

"Not really. Besides, we're supposed to be getting to know each other, aren't we?"

"Oh, before I forget, I've told a few people that we've been corresponding for some time. I had to make a couple of trips to New York in the past year and a half, and I let them think we saw each other then."

Jenny thought for a moment, wondering if she should let him evade her question. He'd quite obviously dodged the issue. But there'd be plenty of time to learn about Alex, she decided. "Why were you in New York?"

"For a conference about six months ago, and before that, I had to take a dog that needed surgery I wasn't equipped to do here."

She smiled. He really was amazing. Kind, smart, dependable and good-looking, too, with those sexy gray eyes. Why couldn't she find a man like him?

She *had* found him.

The thought unnerved her. She couldn't afford to think that way. This arrangement wasn't for keeps. He'd made it clear she was to stay only as long as it took her to recover. He liked his life the way it was and didn't want any entanglements. One of the main reasons the arrangement could work was that he had no plans to marry again. He'd been quite adamant about that.

"What's wrong?" He took her hand and peered at her with endearing concern. "You don't look well."

"I'm fine. But I did eat too much."

"Me, too." He patted his flat stomach.

"What do you do for exercise?"

"Exercise?"

"Yeah, you know, jog, swim, go to the gym."

His mouth curved in a wry smile. "Trying to tell me I'm out of shape?"

She laughed. "Heavens, no. The opposite." She pressed a palm to his stomach, belatedly realizing she shouldn't have done that. Quickly she withdrew her hand and stared at the ground. "Actually, I think you look really good," she murmured, embarrassed as all get out.

"Thanks." He lifted her chin with his index finger and smiled. "As much as I'd like to claim credit, I think genetics and manual labor around the clinic account for any muscle tone I may have."

Heat crept into her cheeks. She didn't blush often. Not anymore. But sitting so close to Alex and having been bold enough to place her hand on his belly had unsettled her. He was nice to show her he didn't mind, but still...

"Remember when Father Tom instructed me to kiss my bride?"

She nodded, her gaze locked with his, her pulse taking a flying leap.

He moved his hand from her chin and slid it around to the back of her neck. "How about if I do my duty now?"

"You mean you want to—" she cleared her throat "—kiss me?"

"Would you mind?" He'd already started moving

forward, and his warm breath skimmed the spot where his finger had been on her chin.

Without waiting for a response, he brushed his lips across hers—lightly, teasing—and then slowly retreated. But before disappointment could fully settle in, he kissed her again, using greater pressure, slanting his head for a more thorough exploration.

She was about to part her lips for him when he pulled back and looked at her. He had the most unreadable expression on his face, as if he were purposely trying to conceal any emotion. "I hope I didn't frighten you."

"Of course not." She hadn't quite caught her breath yet. She wanted him to kiss her again, finish what he'd started. Maybe if she leaned forward, gave him a sign...

"Phyllis was at the window. I didn't want to miss the opportunity."

Disappointment swelled like a balloon inside her. "No problem."

"I figure we'll have to at least act like newlyweds in public sometimes."

"Sure." She swallowed, trying to get her voice to sound normal. To lose the foolish disappointment that refused to let go. This was stupid. She knew the score. This was Alex being a rescuer, helping out the daughter of a friend. Why the heck was she being so sappy?

"I'm sorry. I can see I've upset you."

"That's not true." She laid a casual hand on his arm and stopped herself a split second before she snatched it back. They couldn't spend the next few months walking on eggs around each other. "You haven't upset me. Believe me, it wasn't a hardship to kiss you."

Oh, God. She bit her lip. She hadn't planned on being *that* honest.

His mouth curved in a slow, sexy smile. "That wasn't even my best work."

"Oh, brother." She rolled her eyes heavenward. "Spoken like a true man."

He laughed. "I deserved that."

It was amazing how quickly the tension between them disappeared. Until he stood, offered her a hand and said, "How about we go inside and give them all something to talk about?"

ALEX HAD thought the worst part of the day was wearing the suit. He was so bloody wrong. The torture had just begun, he realized as he sat thigh to thigh with Jenny on the Coopers' sofa. She smelled so good, and her lips were so soft he could barely think of anything else.

Inconspicuously he checked his watch for the third time. Only ten minutes had passed. In another hour they would be able to get away from the party without hurting anyone's feelings. Frankly, he didn't give a damn about tender feelings. This was supposed to be their wedding night. What were these people thinking?

Not that he'd planned a traditional wedding night. Far from it. But the good citizens of Cooper's Corner didn't know that, and he resented being detained so they could have an excuse for a party and satisfy their curiosity. He would've left by now if it weren't for Jenny. She was afraid of appearing ungrateful.

Alex gritted his teeth. What the hell was wrong with him? It wasn't like him to be this moody. He knew everyone meant well.

That is, everyone except him.

He wanted to kiss Jenny again. Right now.

"Isn't that right, Doc?

Jenny nudged his leg.

He snapped out of his musings. "What?"

Phyllis peered at him with annoyance and concern. "You aren't at all yourself. I don't believe you've heard a word I said, have you?"

"Guilty." He slipped an arm around Jenny and hauled her against him. "How do you expect me to pay attention when my beautiful bride is sitting so close?"

Phyllis and Gina Monroe gasped with delight, then Phyllis dabbed at her eyes. "Doc, I never thought I'd see the day when you'd be this happy again. Thank the good Lord."

He didn't dare look at Jenny. She'd stiffened the moment his arm had gone around her. Thankfully she didn't pull away, though. Either she was playing along or she was too tired to resist. He knew the day's activities had worn her out. She'd alternated between looking pale and flushed, and her hands sometimes shook.

Maureen moved in beside Phyllis and winked so

that only Alex could see. "I think it's time we let these lovebirds go home."

"But it's early." Phyllis's gaze went to the grandfather clock in the corner. "We haven't even cut the cake."

Jenny groaned softly.

Alex whispered, "Don't worry, we aren't staying. We'll promise to have some tomorrow."

He was about to make their excuses to Phyllis when Philo took his wife by the arm and said, "Come on. Let them have their privacy. They can eat cake anytime. Tonight is their wedding night, for goodness sakes."

His booming voice carried across the living room into the dining room, stopping conversation and making people look up and laugh. Jenny's face turned pink.

"Well put, Philo." Alex got up and shook the man's hand. "You all go on and have a good time. We'll be thinking about you."

"Right." Philo led everyone in hearty laughter.

"Let's go." He pulled Jenny to her feet.

"Aren't you overdoing the anxious groom bit?" she whispered in annoyance, and then smiled at their audience.

He gave her a quick but hard kiss on the lips. "Say goodbye to everyone, Jenny."

Her eyes widened, and he felt her warm breath come out in a whoosh. "Goodbye everyone."

More laughter.

"I wish you'd warn me before you do things like

that,'' she said in a stern whisper as they stepped outside.

''You think I should ask permission to kiss my wife? At least I got us out of there.'' He jerked open the car door for her. He wasn't sure why, but her words stung.

''I'm sorry. You're right.'' She hesitated getting in and looked at him. ''Alex, I haven't told you how much I appreciate what you're doing. I really—''

''Forget it.'' He continued to hold the door, wishing she'd get in. ''I thought you wanted to go home.''

''Of course.'' She gave him a hurt look then ducked into the car.

He closed the door, then swung around to the driver's side. He'd borrowed the car from Tuck so Jenny wouldn't have to ride the pickup in her linen suit. Across the back end, Tuck and Grace's children had attached a whimsical sign announcing to the world that Alex and Jenny were Just Married.

''Alex?''

He didn't want to talk. ''Yeah?''

''I'm sorry if I upset you.''

''You haven't.'' He slid the key into the ignition and started the engine.

''I know this isn't a real marriage, but we do have to communicate.''

He sighed. ''What's on your mind?''

''Please don't sound so defensive.''

He flinched. Sara used to accuse him of being defensive when she wanted to talk and he didn't. ''I didn't mean to." He took a deep breath and decided to bite the bullet. "It's about the kiss, right?"

"What do you mean?"

"Come on, Jen. Communication goes both ways."

"I'm not trying to be obtuse. I really don't know what you're getting at. I could guess, but that's all."

"Go ahead. Give it your best shot." He put the car in gear and pulled out of the Coopers' driveway.

"But if I'm wrong, I'll be horribly embarrassed."

That piqued his curiosity, and he slid her an inquisitive glance. She quickly turned her head and pretended to look out the window. Except it was too dark to see a thing.

"You know I did that for show, right?"

"Of course."

"Okay, so maybe I was a little too enthusiastic." This was not going well. But at least the reality check cooled off his confused libido. "But it's over. We don't have to prove anything to anyone. We'll probably rarely be out in public together."

"You're misunderstanding."

He pulled to a stop at an intersection. No other cars were on the road, but he waited, turning to look at her. "How so?"

She took a nervous swipe at her hair. "I didn't mean to have this big discussion while you were driving. Maybe we should wait until we get to your house."

Now he was really curious. He didn't even know they were having a "big discussion." But he wouldn't push. She was tired and probably feeling worse than she'd let on. She was a trouper, he'd give her that. "We're only three miles away."

"I remember."

He crossed the intersection. "Not much has changed around here."

"Which is so nice. Comforting, really."

That surprised him. "I thought you didn't like it here. You couldn't wait to leave."

"That was youthful yearning, wondering if the grass was greener on the other side. Besides, I never disliked living here. There just wasn't enough career opportunity."

They lapsed into silence. Alex knew Ed had believed that was the reason his daughter had left, but Alex figured that was a father's rationalization for having been deserted. But Jenny had no reason to lie. This was certainly a new take on things.

The house came into view as soon as they turned down the long drive. He'd switched on several lights, not knowing if they'd come back after the ceremony or go out to dinner. He noticed Jen shift in her seat and wondered what she was thinking. She had to be nervous. This was a strange house and even stranger circumstances.

And he hadn't helped one bit by kissing her. Twice. On the porch and in the living room. In his heart he knew he'd taken advantage of the situation. He could've snuggled up to her, or pulled her closer, and Phyllis would have been satisfied. But he'd let his testosterone overrule his good sense.

He parked the car in the double garage beside the

pickup, and they both got out at the same time. Jenny hesitated near the door that led to the house.

He knew what had drawn her attention.

"By the way, that's some truck."

"I wondered when you'd get around to that." He smiled, used to the ribbing. "Very handy for a vet who makes house calls. My patients' owners know I'm coming from miles away."

"Ah, I see." She smiled back. "Am I to assume purple is your favorite color?"

"No, it was Sara's. She picked it out a year before she died."

"Oh." Jenny blinked, and her smile faded.

He shrugged, but a sharp reminder of the day Sara had announced she wanted a purple truck sprang to mind. He'd balked, but in the end he'd given in. Just as he'd always given in to her. And now he couldn't part with the ugly purple thing. "Honestly, I hated the color. But the truck runs, and I saw no need to get rid of it."

"Of course not." She moistened her lips. "I really wasn't poking fun."

He grinned. "That's okay. It is an ugly color."

"Anyway, I should talk. You've seen my clunker."

He motioned her to precede him to the door. "Practically speaking, how reliable is that car?"

"I haven't had it long. I didn't need it in the city, but a friend sold it to me for a song, and I figured if I—" She shook her head. "It doesn't matter now. It gets me where I'm going."

Alex followed her into the kitchen, mulling over

what she'd said. Had she decided to leave the city? Had she planned on moving back to Cooper's Corner? Ed hadn't said anything. No, that wasn't it. She was sick and hadn't wanted her father to know. Alex could ask her what she'd meant, except if she'd wanted to tell him, she would have done so.

"I think we'd better consider getting you a new, more reliable vehicle," he finally said.

She spun to face him. "Absolutely not. I don't have the money, and you aren't spending a dime of yours on me." She visibly swallowed. "As it is, I'm going to be your indentured servant for the next ten years."

"Hey, knock that off. You don't owe me anything. Understand?"

She didn't answer, but looked away. "Mind if I take a pitcher of water to my room with me?"

"For God's sake, Jenny, you don't have to ask me something like that. You do what you want around here." Annoyed, he threw the keys on the counter. "I'm having a glass of wine. Want one?"

"No, thanks. I think I'll just go on to bed."

He laid a hand on her arm when she turned to go. "I didn't mean to snap at you."

"It's all right. We've had a long day."

"That's still no excuse." He knew why he was irritable. He felt like a heel for scaring her. She probably thought he expected something physical out of the deal.

Should he bring the subject up? Or would that fuel the tension? Maybe she wanted to discuss the terms of their relationship. She'd started a conversation in the car....

"No hard feelings. I promise." She moved away. "But I really am exhausted."

"You started to say something in the car and then decided to wait until we got home."

She stiffened, clearly uncomfortable. "It's really not important, after all."

"I have a feeling it is."

She crossed her arms over her chest and hugged herself as if she were cold.

"Jen, look." He took a step toward her, then thought better of it and stopped. "I know you're still upset about the kiss." She started to protest, but he stopped her. "More accurately, about the direction of our relationship. I want to reassure you, nothing has changed. I expect nothing from you. Am I clear?"

Jenny nodded. It was difficult to maintain eye contact. How could she have been so foolish as to think there might be a mutual attraction? Thank God she'd cut herself off in the car. She would have died if she'd come out and told him she'd liked it when he'd kissed her, that she'd wanted to kiss him back.

He obviously still mourned Sara. He couldn't even get rid of the ugly purple truck.

CHAPTER SIX

THREE WEEKS after the wedding, Jenny finally started to relax. The application to have her added to Alex's medical insurance had been sent on their wedding day, and in that regard, all she could do was wait. Not pleasant, but at least she knew there was a light at the end of the tunnel.

Most of the time she stuck around the house, not knowing how she'd feel each day. She spent her time doing light housework and gardening in spite of Alex's protests. She knew what was in all the cupboards and cabinets and was amazed at how much she liked puttering around the kitchen, trying different recipes. In New York, she'd had little time to cook. Usually she'd picked up sandwiches or eaten canned soup.

Alex was busy at the clinic for sometimes twelve hours at a time, and she really missed him on those days. She missed his touch, too, and wondered if he was purposely staying away. He was always pleasant and even teased her a little, but he wasn't at all like the playful man he'd been at the potluck.

Maybe he regretted the offer. A year was a long time out of someone's life. She understood that only too well. Selfishly, though, she didn't want to press the issue, talk herself into a position where she'd have to offer to back out of the deal. This was her only way to get well, to get her life on track.

This was a gift, a small miracle. The kind they talked about in her support group in New York. She missed the people in her group, a mixture of kooks and intellectuals and average Joes brought together by a common despair. They'd saved her sanity on more than one occasion when she'd felt like giving up, losing all hope, wallowing in self-pity.

The ringing of the phone startled her, and she laid down the dish towel she was using to dry this morning's juice glasses to answer it.

She'd barely got out a hello when Alex said, "I hope you haven't made anything for dinner."

"Actually, I thought we'd have leftover pot roast." She sat at the kitchen table and put her feet up to relieve the pressure on her back. He generally called her twice a day to check up on her, but his requisite calls had already been made. "Why?"

"We're going out to dinner."

At the banked excitement in his voice, her pulse skittered. "What's going on?"

"It's a surprise."

"That's mean."

"Why?"

"I don't like being kept in suspense."

"Poor baby." He chuckled. "You only have to wait two more hours."

Her gaze went to the whimsical cow clock over the

door. It was four. "You're coming home early?" Darn it. She hadn't meant to sound so excited, but the playfulness in his voice had her a little giddy.

He paused. "Yep. If that's all right."

"Of course it is." Her mood deflated. What an odd thing for him to say. Was he purposely staying away because he thought that's what she wanted? She hesitated. "I like having you around."

Silence stretched. "I have to give a poodle his vaccinations and examine a Siamese who seems to think she's a dog, and then I'll be home. I'm guessing an hour."

Jenny let out a relieved breath and smiled. "Good."

"Why? So you won't be in suspense?"

She closed her eyes and blurted, "Because I miss you."

Silence again. And then he said, "I'll give the Siamese a good talking-to and be home in forty minutes."

Without another word, he hung up. Jenny replaced the receiver and stared at the phone, a slow smile spreading across her face.

"WHAT IS THAT?" Jenny stared at the huge green and yellow bird in the cage Alex was carrying into the living room. A parrot or a macaw, she guessed, but it sure was gigantic.

"Not what…but *who*. Otherwise you'll hurt Plato's feelings." Alex hung the cage in the corner of the living room. "Plato's a macaw. I generally leave him at the clinic since I'm there so much, but I brought him home to keep you company.''

''This is my surprise?'' When she realized how that sounded, she quickly added, ''Thank you. That's very thoughtful.''

Alex grinned. ''You don't like birds.''

''I don't know. I never met one before.''

''He'll grow on you.'' He turned to the bird. ''Plato?''

''Alex.''

Jenny gasped. ''He said your name.''

''Plato?'' Alex drawled the bird's name in warning.

''Alex,'' the bird repeated.

''Knock it off.'' He flicked a fingernail against the cage, and Plato let out an annoyed squawk. ''Behave yourself. There's someone I want you to meet. This is Jenny.''

Plato said nothing. He looked around the room... anywhere but at her.

Alex sighed. ''He's being stubborn. Plato?''

''Alex.''

''Okay, that does it.'' He motioned to Jenny for them to leave. ''Let's go to dinner. The little tyrant can sit alone and stew.''

''What about water?'' Jenny wasn't sure if she liked the little bully or not, but she didn't want him to go thirsty.

Alex winked. ''He'll be fine. Let's go.''

They got to the door, and Plato let out a panicked squawk. ''Alex! Alex!''

He slowly turned to the bird. "Are you ready to say hi to Jenny?"

Silence.

"Okay, Jen, let's go." Alex opened the door.

"Alex! Jenny! Alex!"

She gave a startled laugh and stared at Plato in awe. "He said my name."

"Can you say hello?" Alex kept his hand on the doorknob.

"Hello, Jenny." Plato made an otherworldly sound, then repeated, "Hello, Jenny. Hello, Jenny."

"Okay, Plato, enough." Alex shook his head and glanced at Jenny. "Now he has to have the last word. We'll leave for dinner in about twenty minutes. Let him have his little triumph."

She still couldn't believe how the macaw could communicate. He was incredibly articulate. "Does he bite?"

"Let's just say you'd better let him get to know you for a few days before you get too cozy."

The bird eyed them as they talked, as if he were trying to figure out what they were saying. Jenny took a seat on the couch with her back to him. Not that she thought he could actually understand, but still… "What about Bagel? Will he have a problem with Plato staying here?"

Alex sat at the other end of the couch, and swung his long legs toward her. "Plato is around dogs and cats at the clinic. Sometimes he has a temper tantrum and squawks up a storm for a few seconds. If Bagel gets curious or too close, Plato will get rid of him."

"Thank you for bringing him home. It's a great surprise." She still didn't know how she felt about having the bird around. But she appreciated the gesture.

He smiled. "That isn't your surprise."

"Oh."

"This is." He reached into his pocket and pulled out something that looked like a credit card.

"What is it?"

"Here." He handed it to her.

Her eyes widened. It was an insurance card with her name on it. "I've been approved." She raised her gaze to his. "I'm officially insured?"

"Yep."

She put a hand to her throat. "Oh, my God. It finally seems real."

"It's real, all right. You can call Dr. Sage's office tomorrow and set up the appointment to discuss the surgery."

She wanted to cry. She wouldn't, of course—certainly not in front of Alex. "This is so unbelievable. Thank you."

"No more thanking me." He looked pretty emotional himself. "As soon as you get the appointment, I'll take care of our plane tickets and any other details."

She leaned forward and threw her arms around his neck. She couldn't help it. He had to be the nicest man in the world. She hoped she hadn't just scared the daylights out of him.

He put his arms around her and pulled her close.

"I want you well," he whispered. "That's all that's important."

It finally dawned on her what he'd said, and she straightened to look at him. "You said *our* plane tickets."

"That's right."

"You're coming to New York with me?"

His eyebrows dipped in a frown. "Of course."

"You can't. What about the clinic?"

"I have a partner, remember?"

"But—but..." She shook her head. "I don't expect you to baby-sit me. You've done so much already."

His expression tightened. "I'm not going to baby-sit you, but I am going."

"But I feel awful keeping you away from—"

"Jenny."

"I'll be fine by myself," she continued when he tried to cut her off. "I've been doing research on the computer and I think I understand—"

"Jenny," he said again, this time with impatience.

"Jenny! Jenny! Hello, Jenny." Plato flapped his wings excitedly.

"Not now, Plato." Alex muttered a mild oath. "Look, Jenny—"

"Jenny! Hello, Jenny!"

"Damn it, Plato."

Jenny burst out laughing. "You're not going to win this round."

Alex stared at her with an annoyed expression, then

his lips started to curve. "You two start ganging up on me and I'm taking him back to the clinic."

She grinned. "No, you won't."

His left brow went up. "I won't?"

She shook her head, unable to lose the smile. "You're a big softie, Dr. McAlester."

"You think so, huh?"

"I know so."

He pursed his lips and nodded thoughtfully, his eyes glittering with amusement. "You may change your mind about that. Just try talking me out of accompanying you to New York."

At his intimate tone, she shivered. The thing was, she wanted him to go. But she'd never dreamed he would. She certainly would never have asked it of him. "I won't say anything more about it." She whispered, because that's all her vocal cords were capable of.

"Good, because it would be wasted breath." He brushed a strand of hair from her face, then cupped his hand over her nape. "Ready to go to dinner?"

She hesitated, not wanting to ruin the bond growing between them. But she hadn't realized how much she'd craved his touch until now. His warm palm pressed to her skin was like a balm, a magic elixir.

While she wanted like crazy to break their eye contact, she stayed focused on him. "I'd rather stay here."

He studied her face with undisguised curiosity. "Okay," he said slowly. "We can do that."

She gave him a shy smile and moved a little closer.

He took his hand away from her nape, and she sucked in a breath. God, she'd ruined everything.

"Come here," he said, sliding his arm around her shoulders and urging her closer.

Relieved and too excited for her own good, she snuggled against him and laid her head on his chest. "We have leftovers."

"I'm not hungry. Are you?"

She shook her head.

"Good." He hugged her and kissed the top of her hair. "We'll eat later." He ran a slow, sensual hand down her back. "Much later."

AN HOUR LATER, Jenny was still asleep on Alex's chest. He didn't mind. He was upset with how much she tried to do each day. She pushed herself too hard. For no reason. She could laze around and read or watch television all day. Didn't she understand how sick she was?

Her soft sigh drifted to him, and he closed his eyes, reveling in the sensation of her warm body tucked against him. He'd wanted to kiss her earlier. That he'd dug up enough self-control to keep his mouth from hers amazed him.

The past week had felt like Christmas mornings when he was a kid growing up not far from Cooper's Corner. The present from Santa sat near the tree, tempting, taunting, begging to be opened, but not before his grandparents arrived.

Brutal. Downright brutal.

The only thing that stopped him from kissing her

was that he knew this was what she needed—the snuggling, the closeness, the human connection, not anything sexual.

It pleased him that she wanted him to go with her to New York. Although she'd tried to dissuade him, he'd seen the relief and gratitude in her eyes.

Gratitude. That's all she felt toward him. That's all he should expect. But something was waking him up at night and making him edgy at the clinic during the day. It couldn't be about sex or the lack thereof. He was too old for that sort of nonsense. Not for the sex part, but for acting like a hormonal teenager because she was in the next room.

She stirred against him, and he shifted to make sure she was comfortable. His arm had gone numb from being still so long, but the tingling that would come was a small price to pay to have her close and safe.

God, he hated to consider it, but he wondered how much his feelings for Jen had to do with the fact he'd been unable to help Sara. The strong protectiveness he felt toward Jenny went beyond normal. His powerlessness frustrated and astonished him.

Or maybe this jumble of emotions had to do with Ed. A simple case of transference. Alex couldn't do anything for Jenny's father, so he tried to compensate for his failure by helping her. Not that he had had anything to do with Ed's death or could have foreseen the heart attack. But the mind could be a baffling foe.

He lightly kissed the top of her head and breathed in the peach scent that clung to her hair. When she stirred again, he loosened his arm from around her.

He flexed his left shoulder, and the tingling started, traveling to his wrist. He didn't care. For now she was safe, and tomorrow they'd move forward.

His partner, Tuck, knew what to expect and was prepared to take over the clinic for the time off Alex needed. He had so many questions for Jenny's doctor that he'd been tempted to call the office. But he had a feeling that would've ticked Jen off. In fact, he knew it would make her mad.

He smiled. She was so different from Sara, more opinionated and independent. It could be frustrating sometimes, because she didn't seem to take her condition seriously enough.

She yawned and arched her back. Her breasts pressed against his chest, sending his thoughts in a totally new direction. Her lashes fluttered, then she opened her eyes and looked around as if she'd forgotten where she was.

"Hi."

She stared at him in surprise. "I fell asleep."

He nodded.

Straightening away from him, she put a hand to her hair. Her ponytail had loosened, leaving a mass of flyaway tendrils. "I'm so sorry."

"Don't be. You obviously needed the rest."

"You stayed here the whole time?"

"Yep."

Her cheeks got pink. "You should have just pushed me over to the other side of the couch."

He grinned. "How about something to eat?"

She nodded absently, pulled the pink elastic from

her hair and redid her ponytail, her thoughts clearly miles away. "You did tell me I'm covered by insurance, right? I didn't dream it."

He tucked a strand of hair she'd missed behind her ear. "It's not a dream."

"I guess there was a part of me that was afraid it wouldn't happen. The insurance company would find some snafu that would rule out my coverage."

"No need to worry now."

She sighed and started to relax against him. But a second later she stiffened and moved away, clasping her hands in her lap.

That bothered him, and he got up. "I'll go heat up the leftovers."

"I'll do it." She followed him to the kitchen. "You worked all day. It's the least I can do."

"For goodness sakes, Jen, I don't expect you to be a housekeeper around here." He immediately regretted his curt tone.

It didn't seem to bother her. She glared at him. "We've been through that, if you recall. I need to feel useful."

"Fine." She was right. They'd been down that road before, and she was no less stubborn about it now. He opened the refrigerator and poked around the plastic containers, looking for the leftover pot roast.

She nudged him aside and grabbed a covered blue dish. "Maybe you should have had a nap, too," she muttered.

"What's that supposed to mean?"

She hesitated, then slid him a sideways glance. "You're a grouch."

"No, I'm not."

"Yes, you are, and I don't understand why."

He brought plates from the cabinet and put them on the kitchen table. "I've been in a pretty good mood, actually."

"Until now."

"What did I do?"

She gave him a dry look as she slid the pot roast into the microwave.

"Okay, so I was a little abrupt," he conceded. "That hardly makes me a grouch."

She didn't respond, but placed utensils and napkins near the plates. Next she got out salad fixings. "By the way, I'm not ignoring you," she finally said. "I'm thinking."

He didn't like the sound of that. Better she ignored him.

"Can you get me that yellow bowl, please?" She pointed to the top shelf of the cupboard.

He reached over her, annoyed at the feeling her nearness created. She took the bowl from him then turned to face him. He should have stepped back to give her some space. He didn't.

She tilted her head to look him in the eyes and gave him a sweet smile. "I appreciate what you're doing more than you'll ever know. But you can't hover over me. I know my own body. I know when I push too hard and when I have to rest. It's upsetting to think that on top of having your life disrupted, you're wasting energy worrying about me, too.''

"Wasting energy?''

She laid a hand on his arm. "Keeping a positive outlook is important. Believe me, I've learned the hard way.'' She raised herself on tiptoe and kissed his cheek. "I'm so grateful to you, Alex. I don't want to put you out any more than I have.''

Damn it. That was the problem. He was starting to want more than her gratitude.

CHAPTER SEVEN

ALEX CHECKED his watch as he paced the corridor for the hundredth time. He avoided looking in the rooms, but the smells, the sounds made him feel trapped. Each beep from a monitor, every whiff of antiseptic brought memories of Sara's last days. He did his best to focus on Jenny, on believing she was going to be fine. But the surgery was supposed to take four hours. It had already been five.

The waiting room was empty for the moment, and for that he was grateful. Normally, he didn't mind the idle chitchat of strangers, but not today. He dug into his pocket for change. Another cup of the putrid vending-machine coffee would probably do him in. His stomach was a mess. It didn't matter. He just wanted to hear that Jenny was all right.

Less than two months she'd been with him, and already his emotional investment in her had mounted. Considering all the time they'd spent together in the evenings, playing board games or discussing books they'd read, it was no surprise how much he'd gotten to know and like her. But the whole idea of getting too close still scared him. He wanted her well. He just didn't want to care so damn much.

"Dr. McAlester?"

He looked up to see the surgeon approaching, his face expressionless. Alex's heart slammed against his chest. Why wasn't the guy smiling? He would be smiling if everything were okay.

"We just finished with your wife."

"Just tell me if she's all right."

Dr. Sage's eyebrows went up in surprise. "Of course. She's fine."

Alex let out a shaky breath. "The surgery was a success?"

"Absolutely."

"No complications?"

"A minor one...that's what took us longer than expected. Why don't you sit down?"

"Why? What do you have to tell me? The tumor was malignant?"

The doctor smiled. "No, we never expected it to be. I just don't want you passing out on me."

Alex snorted. "I'm not going to pass out. Can I see her?"

"Not at the moment. They're wheeling her into recovery now."

"Right." Alex decided to sit down, after all.

Dr. Sage sat beside him on the plastic bench. "The tumor was tricky to remove, but I don't anticipate any permanent nerve damage. We were lucky."

Alex listened with half an ear as the doctor gave him details about the surgery. He was so damn grateful and relieved. She was fine. Jenny was going to leave the hospital.

"We've already discussed the kind of physical therapy she'll need over the next six months. And of course I'll meet with both of you again to go over it later. But right now I have to prepare for another patient."

"I understand." Alex stood and shook the doctor's hand. He was one of the three best surgeons in the country for precisely this type of operation. Alex had done extensive research on the man, and he trusted him. "Thank you."

The doctor nodded. "You should be able to see her within the hour. Although don't expect much. She'll still be groggy."

Alex knew that. He just wanted to see her for himself. He wanted to be there when her eyes opened. She probably wouldn't even remember, but that wasn't the point. He just wanted to see her.

Since that wasn't going to happen immediately, he went to the rest room and splashed his face with cold water, then used his cell phone to call Maureen Cooper as he'd promised. He didn't want her worrying needlessly about Jenny. Maureen hadn't been herself lately, probably from the shock of finding Ed Taylor dead.

After he'd made the call and Maureen assured him she would spread the word about Jenny, Alex headed to the downstairs gift shop for flowers. Jen would probably end up in ICU for a day or two, which meant she couldn't have flowers in the room, but hell, he didn't care. He was just so damn glad the surgery was over and a success that he'd give the bouquets to the nurses.

Jenny was going to be okay. The struggle was by no means over. A lot of physical therapy lay ahead, and there would probably be days when she'd wonder why she got up in the morning. But as the months went by, she'd regain her strength and would soon be back to normal.

Alex took a deep breath of bittersweet relief. After she was well again, she'd leave him.

JENNY'S NORMALLY high threshold for pain was crumbling by the minute. Finally, she broke down, sent Alex on a fool's errand and rang for the nurse. As much as she hated taking the pain medication, she couldn't bear another hour of gritting her teeth so as not to alarm Alex.

"Yes, hon, what can I do for you?" Colleen was Jenny's favorite of the three nurses she'd had over the past two days.

"Drugs. I need drugs—and hurry."

Colleen shook her head as she checked Jenny's chart. "I've told you more than once that you shouldn't wait until the pain is this bad before you ask for medication."

"It's not that bad. I want you to hurry and give it to me before Alex gets back."

Close to sixty, Colleen had short salt-and-pepper hair and a round, smiling face. "Your husband does dote on you. It makes my heart glad, to tell you the truth. Every woman should have a man love her the way that man adores you.''

Jenny didn't know what to say to that. She couldn't very well explain to Colleen that she was mistaken, that Alex was really only a friend. ''I hate to rush you but—''

''All right, all right. I'll make it back before that big handsome husband of yours returns.'' The nurse made a notation on the chart, then left to get the medication.

Jenny smiled. He was handsome, that was for sure. He didn't always remember to shave before he came to the hospital in the morning. The stubbly look was incredibly appealing on him, and the polo shirts he favored showed off his nicely muscled arms. He hadn't gotten a haircut in a while, and she really liked the longer look.

The nurses and aides loved to flirt with him. He just smiled a lot, but she could tell he was uncomfortable with all the female attention, even though they meant no harm. Except for one young blond nurse Jenny didn't like. She thought Becky was a tad too eager to see Alex coming.

It wasn't Jenny's imagination that the younger woman applied fresh lipstick five minutes before the start of visiting hours or that she hung around outside Jenny's room at key times. It wasn't that Jenny was jealous. Not in the least. Why would she be? It was just downright annoying to see the nurse acting like that.

''Here we go. This should fix you up in no time.''

Colleen administered the medication. "The doctor will be by to see you within an hour. Maybe he'll be able to tell you when you can go home."

"This afternoon won't be too soon."

"What? You don't like the accommodations?" Colleen grinned. "Don't hold your breath. I'd say you'd be lucky to be released by the end of the week."

"Did I miss something? Has the doctor been here?" Alex asked as he entered the room carrying a white paper sack from the gift shop.

Colleen winked at Jenny. "No, sir. Your wife and I are doing some guesswork." She eyed the bag. "I hope you brought chocolate."

"You know better." He smiled as he reached into the bag. "That stuff will clog your arteries."

"So, we all have to go some time." Colleen grinned.

Jenny watched with unwarranted pride. She knew as well as Colleen that he'd bought the woman some kind of treat. He'd been very generous with all the nurses, bringing everything from bagels and pastries to umbrellas when it rained unexpectedly.

He handed Jenny a small stuffed bear holding a red foil-wrapped chocolate heart. "In case I missed last Valentine's day," he said with a secret smile only for Jenny, and her heart fluttered.

Colleen nudged him with a light elbow to the ribs. "Go on. You've never missed an occasion in your life." She craned her neck. "What else have you got in there?"

"If I tell you, will you go away so I can be alone with my wife?"

Jenny got a warm funny feeling inside even though she knew he'd said that only for show. But there was something in his expression and tone that was so intimate it fueled her foolish imagination.

Colleen frowned at the unhurried way he reached into the bag. "Depends how good it is." Her eyes widened at the gold box he produced. "Holy smoke, Godiva?"

He handed her the box. "This is for *all* of you at the nurses' station, okay?"

Colleen gave him a wicked smile. "I'm glad we're shorthanded today."

"Good-bye, Colleen." He motioned toward the door.

"Keep this up and we'll make sure Jenny never gets discharged," she said over her shoulder.

Jenny groaned. "Gee, thanks."

Alex pulled a chair up beside her bed. He hated the safety bars, even when they were lowered. He hated the monitors, the IV bags. Damn it, he hated hospitals. But he smiled at Jenny, not wanting her to see a hint of his distaste. "How are you feeling?"

"Great." Her pulse sped up when he took her hand and kissed the back of it. "You spoil those nurses."

"I want to make sure they take good care of you."

"Can't wait for me to get back on my feet so you can get rid of me?"

His features tightened and he released her hand. "Is that what you think?"

"I was only joking." She hugged the stuffed bear closer, not sure what to make of Alex's reaction. He'd been so supportive and attentive, it frightened her. She didn't want his attention to end. "Thank you for Romeo."

Alex frowned, then glanced at the bear. "You named him already?"

She nodded. "It was easy. I knew his name as soon as I saw him." She looked at the growing collection of plush bears sitting on the windowsill. "Alex, you've got to quit spoiling me, too."

"Why?"

"Because."

His lips curved in a slow smile. "I see."

The pain medication had started to kick in, and she was feeling slightly fuzzy-headed. "I don't want you spending your money like this. Airfare, cab fare, meals, phone calls, it's all adding up. And what about the clinic? Have you called Tuck and—"

He silenced her with a finger to her lips. "Don't worry. Everything is fine. Your only job is to get well."

"That would be okay if I were really your wife but—"

"You are my wife."

"You know what I mean." She lay back and closed her eyes. It was humbling enough to have to lie here, no makeup, barely any modesty, having to depend on everyone to do things for her. Even harder was to watch Alex play the role of loving husband.

"Hey." He stroked her arm. "What's wrong?"

"I don't know." She sniffed. "I feel so helpless."

"It's temporary. You'll get stronger and stronger, and before you know it, you'll be back on your feet, and then..." His voice faded.

Curious, she opened her eyes and looked at him, waiting for him to finish.

He shrugged. "And you'll be back to your job and your old life in the city."

She swallowed. That was part of the problem. The thought no longer appealed to her. She wanted to stay with Alex, which was a foolish idea to even consider right now. She was vulnerable and grateful—of course she wanted to stay where she felt safe. Her growing attachment to him was probably right out of a psychology textbook.

Heck, it was foolish to consider a relationship with him at any time. Hadn't Alex made it clear he would never remarry? That no one could replace Sara? That's why he'd said this arrangement could work. There would never be a romantic interest in his life. He couldn't have been plainer that this was a short-term arrangement.

"Jen?"

Oh, God, she hoped she didn't do anything stupid like start crying. She swallowed hard. "Yes?"

"You look as if you've just lost your best friend. What's wrong?"

Damn it. There wasn't a thing she could do about the sudden gush of tears.

He jumped up. "I'll get the nurse."

"No, don't." She barely choked out the words. "She can't help."

Confusion and fear darkened his face. "Honey, please tell me what's wrong."

She hiccuped. "My hormones are out of whack or something. That's all."

His expression softened. "It's okay to be emotional. Your body's been through a lot of trauma."

She nodded. "Could I please have a tissue?"

He got the box from her bedside table and put it next to her on the bed. "You're not withholding anything from me, are you?"

She blew her nose a little too loudly. "Like what?"

"Like not wanting to tell me you're in pain."

"No." She waved a hand. "It's just stupid stuff. I'm fine. In fact, I'm hoping the doctor will tell me I can go home in a couple of days."

"Don't push it. Remember, home is a few hundred miles away."

"You haven't given up my apartment yet."

"No, I've paid the rent through the end of the month and given written notice that you're vacating then." He wiped a stray tear off her cheek. "It really doesn't make sense to keep it once we go back to Cooper's Corner."

Jenny dabbed at her eyes. She must look a complete mess.

He plucked a tissue from the box and handed it to her. "You can get an apartment that's just as nice after you've recuperated."

"Just as nice?" Jenny gave him a wry smile.

"You're being much too charitable. I was almost too embarrassed to agree that you stay there while I'm in here. But it made sense financially."

"It's small but big enough for one person, and it seems relatively safe. Besides, this is the city. Square footage is expensive."

She sighed. "Yeah. Everything's a trade-off here."

"You'll be back sooner than you think."

She frowned. She wished he'd quit saying things like that. It sounded as if he was anxious to be rid of her. Of course she couldn't blame him. After all, she'd turned his life upside down.

"You look tired." He peered intently at her as if he were examining one of his canine patients. "Maybe I should leave for a while and let you rest."

"And disappoint your fan club?" She let her eyes drift closed for a second. The medication made her groggy.

"Huh?"

"The nurses."

"I bring them chocolate. What do you expect?"

"No, I think it's your charm and big hands."

He laughed. "Big hands?"

Oh, God. Had she actually said that out loud? More than one fantasy about those large, strong, capable hands had kept her awake at night. "I didn't mean that. I guess I am a little tired."

He lifted one of her lids and studied her pupil. "Did they give you more Vicodin?"

She nodded. Better he knew than think she was a total dope.

He let his fingers trail down her cheek. "I wish you'd tell me when you're uncomfortable."

"Then you'll argue about me going home."

"I only want what's best for you," he said softly, smoothing her hair.

"We all do." Dr. Sage walked in, a tired smile on his round face. "How are you doing today, Jennifer?"

"Better."

"Good honest answer." He nodded at Alex before concentrating on her chart.

Jenny held her breath, suddenly a little more alert. She wanted so badly to go home. Not just to her apartment. But to Cooper's Corner. To Alex's home.

"All right," the doctor said slowly. "Everything looks pretty good here." He mumbled some vital statistics from her chart that had Alex looking pleased.

She sighed, wishing he'd get to the bottom line. But she knew better than to rush him. She'd tried that before and ended up with him and Alex ganging up on her.

Dr. Sage set down the chart. "I think I'd better take a look at that incision."

Jenny stiffened when he pushed aside her hospital gown. Alex was still in the room, although from where he stood he couldn't see much.

Dr. Sage smiled. "You don't mind if your husband stays in the room, do you?"

The question was obviously rhetorical. He'd already exposed her lower back and half her fanny. She closed her eyes and exhaled slowly. This was not how she'd planned on Alex seeing her naked.

"You're healing quite nicely." He gently prodded the area. "Can you feel this?"

"Yes."

"Some patients experience a little numbness when we get that close to the nerve. Eventually the feeling comes back, but you're doing great."

"How bad will the scar be?" She'd thought about asking Colleen for a small mirror to see the damage but had chickened out.

Dr. Sage covered her with the gown. "Not bad at all. You and your husband will hardly notice it unless you wear one of those thong bikinis."

"That is *so* not going to happen." Jenny avoided Alex's gaze even when she heard him chuckle.

"Do you have any questions?" the doctor asked, picking up the chart again.

"Just one."

He looked at her with raised eyebrows.

"When do I get to leave?"

"What's wrong? You don't like the food?" Dr. Sage grinned. "Sorry. A little hospital humor." He went back to studying the chart for a moment. "I hope you're not planning on traveling back to Massachusetts immediately."

"No." Alex jumped in, his tone firm. "Definitely not. We'll be staying here in the city for as long as we need to."

Although Jenny had thought about taking a train, which would allow her to leave sooner, Jenny gritted her teeth but she didn't argue. She figured the more agreeable she was, the better her chances were of getting released.

"Well..." Dr. Sage pursed his lips and appeared thoughtful. "You're doing better than expected. How does tomorrow sound?"

"Tomorrow? Really?"

Alex shook his head. "That's awfully soon."

"Tell me, young fellow." The doctor gave him an amused look. "You like it when your patients' masters second-guess you?"

Alex sighed. "Point taken."

"Can I leave first thing tomorrow?" Jenny asked, impatient to confirm her release date.

"After we discuss a schedule with the physical therapist. Who are you working with?"

"Olga Mendez."

"Good. While you're in New York, you'll continue working with her twice a day. In two weeks we should be able to cut the sessions back to three days a week."

Jenny groaned. "Does that mean I have to stay here for two more weeks?"

Dr. Sage exchanged a concerned look with Alex. "You're healing well and you obviously have a lot of physical resilience," he told Jenny. "Unfortunately, that's a two-edged sword. You'll want to push yourself and do too much too soon. I see patients make that mistake all the time, and then they end up back in here."

She shuddered at the thought. "Don't worry. I'll be as good as gold."

"Yes, she will." Alex moved closer to the bed. "I'll see to it."

She didn't much care for his patronizing attitude, but if it helped get her sprung, she could deal with it. "How long will I have to continue to use the walker?"

"For at least two weeks. And that is definitely not negotiable." Dr. Sage gave her a pointed look. "Young people especially hate using it, but I promise you, young lady, you won't be able to walk without it no matter how hard you try, and you'll only end up in this bed again."

She smiled meekly. "Of course I'll use it." And she meant it. During her last trip to the bathroom, she'd learned the hard way how dependent she was on the walker. That's why she'd had to have more pain medication.

Still, she hated using it in front of Alex. She always made sure she went to the bathroom before he came to see her, and she wouldn't allow him to watch her physical therapy sessions. Foolish. Why should she care if he saw her hobbling like an old lady?

"By the end of the two weeks, you'll probably be able to get by with a cane. I've arranged for you to continue your therapy at the hospital in Cooper's Corner. Stick with the program and you'll be good as new in no time." The doctor looked at his watch and then at Alex. "Either of you have any more questions?"

"Not at the moment, but I'm sure I will later," Alex said. Jenny figured she ought to be angry with him for taking over, except his hand had found hers, and the way he stroked the inside of her wrist drove her crazy.

"Good enough." Dr. Sage patted the blanket over her knee. "I'll see you during my rounds early tomorrow morning, and you should be out of here by ten."

Jenny waited until he disappeared into the hall. "Yahoo!"

"Hey, don't get too excited."

"You haven't had to lie here and get poked and prodded every few hours."

"I know." He squeezed her hand. "But it's over. The worst part, anyway."

She nodded, a sudden rush of tears filling her eyes. "Thank you, Alex."

"So help me, if you thank me one more time, I'll—"

She sniffed. "You'll what?"

He studied her for a moment, then dipped his head and kissed her.

CHAPTER EIGHT

ALEX WATCHED Jenny struggle with the walker, the helpless frustration in her face burning a hole in his gut. It hadn't been an easy week for her. Just getting from the apartment to physical therapy wore her out. She never complained, though, not even once.

He forced his attention to the medical record Tuck had faxed him. Gertrude Whynot's collie had another urinary tract infection, the third one this year without reason. Alex had to be missing something.

Jen made it halfway to the kitchen and sat down, her expression grim.

"May I get you anything?" he asked casually, knowing her answer would be no. Sometimes she was too independent and stubborn for her own good.

She wrinkled her nose. "Yeah."

He immediately rose. This was a first.

"I'd like a double cheeseburger from the Burger Barn."

That startled a laugh out of him. "They have a Burger Barn here?"

She shook her head. "I wonder if they still make the monster burger with the Thousand Island dressing and extra pickles. Oh, and their onion rings are to die for. And their fries. Not the regular ones...the spicy curly ones.''

With a groan she sank back in the chair, made a face and shifted to a more comfortable position, angling slightly on her side.

"You're talking about the Burger Barn outside Cooper's Corner, I assume."

"The one and only. I spent half my teen years there. Oh, God, their shakes. I almost forgot about their awesome double chocolate shakes."

Alex laughed. "You like torturing yourself like this?"

"No offense, but I am sick of soup and salad."

"Hey, you're the one who said you had to eat light since you weren't getting enough exercise. I'd be happy to make you something else."

She grinned. "Make something else? As in open a different can of soup?"

"I never said I could cook."

"No, you didn't," she agreed. "Because that would have been a big fat lie."

"Who went out in the rain to get you hot and sour soup from Chang's five blocks away?"

Her eyes lit up. "Have I told you how much I appreciate you? How crazy I am about you? How much I adore and worship you?" She paused. "How much I'd love another bowl of that hot and sour soup?"

Shaking his head in mock annoyance, he got to his feet and felt his back pocket for his wallet. Amazing how she never lost her sense of humor. No matter how tired or frustrated or in pain she was, she always had a smile or something positive to say.

Sara had been so somber all the time. Of course, she knew she was dying. But even before they knew about the cancer, there'd never been much laughter.

Damn it. He did not want to think about Sara or compare the two women. It wasn't fair. Not to them. Not to him.

"Alex?"

He dismissed his troubling thoughts and met Jen's concerned eyes.

"I didn't mean for you to go right now. In fact, you don't have to go at all. We still have some chicken noodle."

"I don't mind going. The walk will do me good."

She bit her lower lip. "I hope you don't think I take you for granted. I truly don't. I—"

"The thought never crossed my mind. If anything, I wish you'd let me do more for you."

"You've done too much already, but I swear I'll make this all up to you."

"Stop it, Jen. For God's sake, you're my wife."

She drew her head back in surprise.

Hell, he'd surprised himself. "Yeah, I know, in name only."

The phrase annoyed him more than it had before. This past week they'd been together constantly, doing everything a married couple would do, like reading the paper together, jockeying for the remote control.

They ate together, laughed and talked and read a lot of the same books, which had resulted in several spirited discussions. She was very liberal, he'd discovered, much more than he was.

But the bottom line was, they slept separately. She slept in her bed, and he took the couch. That was as it should be. But he didn't have to like it.

Not that he planned on anything amorous. Her surgery had barely been two weeks ago, and she was in no shape for any new adventures.

Jenny cleared her throat. "To be perfectly honest, I'm not quite sure how to take that remark."

"I don't know." That was another interesting thing about her. She didn't gloss over uncomfortable topics. She met them head-on, an admirable characteristic that alternately fascinated and irritated him.

"I don't blame you for getting tired of the setup. Maybe tonight you should go see a play, have a drink at the Plaza or Saint Moritz. Maybe you'll meet someone nice." Her voice broke, but she gave him a reassuring smile.

"I don't want to go out alone. I don't want to meet anyone. Nice or otherwise."

She blinked. "I just thought maybe—well, you looked so disgusted."

"I'm not disgusted." He ran a hand through his hair. Man, it was getting long. Tomorrow he'd get it cut. "I just want to go get the soup, okay?"

She shrugged. "Okay."

The way she seemed to shrink into the chair cushions made him feel like a heel. He should explain, tell her he didn't feel tied down to her but just the opposite. He thought about touching her and kissing her all the time. He wanted to taste her so badly, the desire kept him up at night.

But what purpose would it serve to admit that to her? The knowledge would only make her uncomfortable around him. To put her in that position would be cruel. She still depended on his emotional and financial support and would need to do so for the next eight or ten months.

"Look, Jen, I don't regret our arrangement. I'm not bored, disgusted, unhappy, any of those things. Okay?"

She nodded, her smile failing miserably.

But he couldn't do anything about it without creating more tension. So he grabbed the apartment key and headed out, the rejection on her face haunting him for five blocks.

"WHAT'S A three-letter word for double over?"

Alex glanced up from the sports section of the newspaper, looking so handsome Jenny's heart fluttered. He hadn't shaven, and his hair was tousled. She was glad he hadn't had it cut yet. The rugged look suited him.

He frowned briefly. "Ply."

"Really?"

"I think so."

"Ply, huh?" She checked the words going down the puzzle. "It'll work. How did you know that?"

"Toilet paper. Two-ply means double tissue."

"Oh." No way would she have been able to think

that quickly. Alex was exceptionally bright. "Thanks."

She focused on the crossword puzzle until she knew he'd returned to reading the newspaper. And then she raised her gaze to study the way the morning sunlight filtered through the bay window to touch the blond highlights in his hair.

Even his beard had some blond in it. No gray yet. Not that she could see. He'd turned forty at the beginning of the year, she recently discovered, and she smiled. Forty used to sound so ancient.

Alex didn't seem old at all. His grave sense of responsibility spoke of his maturity, though, and he was analytical and exact. No impulsive decisions for him. He thought problems through until he came up with a solution—an acceptable solution and not merely one that would let him off the hook or enable him to ignore the problem.

It would be only too easy to lay herself at his mercy. Let him make her decisions for her. He'd never steer her wrong, at least not intentionally. Or hurt her. She'd bet everything she owned on that belief.

Not that she owned anything worth spit. The tan Italian leather sofa she'd splurged on after moving to New York was the nicest piece of furniture in the apartment. Good thing, too, because at least she knew Alex was relatively comfortable at night.

Surely more comfortable than she'd been the past week, lying there for hours wishing he were next to her. But that wasn't likely to happen, since he practically made a point of steering clear of her unless he was helping her get into the elevator or a cab.

Several times she thought about pretending to faint just to force him to touch her, but she could clearly see how that would backfire. He'd probably delay their planned trip home at the end of the week.

How easily she thought of Alex's place as home. Much more so than this tiny excuse for an apartment. And not because of the size. She'd grown used to cramped quarters after moving to the city. Besides, until a year ago she'd worked so many long hours she was rarely home.

The simple fact was, the apartment wasn't a home. There were no handmade pillows or hooked rugs like the ones at Alex's house. The two Leroy Newman prints on the wall were attractive and contemporary and a little pricey, but they didn't compare to the watercolors of wildflowers in Alex's two-story homey brick colonial.

She sighed. Other than the sofa and the prints, she really didn't much care what they did with the things she'd picked up in thrift stores and through the classifieds.

Alex looked up from the paper. "You bored?"

"No, I still have three books of crosswords to do. Why would I be bored?"

He smiled and put down the paper. "Is that what all that sighing is about?"

She sighed again. "I didn't realize I was doing that out loud."

"How about another game of Scrabble?"

"No, thanks. I don't think my ego can take being beaten four times in one day."

"I'll let you win."

She glared at him. "Don't you ever do that." She put down the pen and stared closely at him. "Did you let me win that third game of backgammon?"

"Nope."

"You swear?"

"I was teasing when I said I'd let you win at Scrabble. I'd never insult you that way. Besides, you're perfectly capable of beating me on your own."

Appeased, she went back to studying her puzzle. She believed him. Not because of the indignation on his face but because Alex was too honorable and straightforward to be so childish as to let her win a silly game.

Right?

She looked at him. "What about chess yesterday?"

He smiled. "What about it?"

"Did you give me a handicap?"

"I see. You're trying to get me to admit that you really cleaned my clock."

She tried to tamp down a triumphant smile. "I wouldn't go that far."

"Right."

"Hey, I just wanted to make sure you hadn't given me any unfair advantage because I was so down yesterday."

He frowned. "I didn't know—what was wrong?"

"Nothing, really. Probably a little cabin fever."

She shrugged. "I'm not used to being so inactive. Hey, I've got an idea."

He narrowed his gaze. "Yes?"

"After physical therapy this afternoon, we're going on a little field trip."

"What?" Alex shook his head. "After therapy, we come straight home like always."

"Not today." The thought cheered her immensely.

"Jenny, be sensible. You're always exhausted after therapy."

"What I have planned won't be strenuous. I promise."

"What is it?"

No way would she spill the beans. He'd only tell her to forget it. She gave him a mischievous smile. "It's a surprise."

"OH, LOOK AT HER. Isn't she beautiful."

Alex shook his head. "This isn't a good idea."

Jenny ignored him. Using her walker for support, she reached up to stroke the horse's nose. "I think she's the one."

The mare was a beauty, all right, even wearing the undignified straw hat with fake purple flowers. Her chocolate brown coat glistened like silk in the sun, and her liquid brown eyes were entirely too persuasive.

"I've lived in this city for over two years and never taken a carriage ride through Central Park. I kept saying I would but I'd always get too busy." Jenny looked at the horse's owner. He had a gold hoop earring in each ear and one in his left eyebrow. "How much is it?"

Before the man could answer, Alex stepped in. "Give us a minute."

The guy shrugged and went back to shelling peanuts and popping them in his mouth.

Alex put a hand on her shoulder, sympathy in his eyes. "Going for a carriage ride is a great idea. And when you're well, I think we should do it. But right now it's too risky."

"Risky? I've been riding New York cabs to therapy for the past week and a half, and you call this risky?"

"The pathway is uneven, and there are too many bumps. And no matter how well trained, a horse can be unpredictable. I really think—"

"Alex…"

"—that you should wait until—"

"Alex." This time her tone was stern.

"What?"

"I appreciate your concern and all the great care you've taken of me. Really, I do. But I'm not asking your permission to take this carriage ride." Her expression softened. "I am going on the ride, and I'd like it if you came with me."

Alex rubbed his tired eyes. Damn, she was stubborn. "What if—"

She shook her head. "There is no negotiation here."

"I don't understand you, Jen. Usually you're so sensible."

"You're right. I am sensible, so trust me. I know my own body. I know what I can handle and what I can't. You'll have to trust that I do."

Alex sighed. Why did she have to go and put it that way? "Of course I'll go with you."

Her smile lit her eyes. "Thanks. Is Daisy okay with you?"

"Daisy?"

She glanced at the mare. On the side of her hat, the name was stitched in red.

"What a name for a horse," he muttered, and signaled to the owner.

Jenny laughed. "Tell Bagel and Plato that."

"Those are two great names."

"Just teasing." She grinned, and using the walker slowly moved to the back of the carriage.

He watched her with mixed feelings. While he worried she was being too impulsive, pushing herself as the doctor had warned against, Alex admired her resilience. She had a lot of spirit, a joy of life that was often lacking in people who'd been ill for a while.

Of course she was on the mend, which would account for much of her exuberance, but Jenny had been a fighter from the beginning. He doubted he would have known she was sick if she hadn't fainted at the funeral. Hell, she hadn't even told Ed.

"Uh, Alex, I'm afraid I'm going to need some help up." Jenny had one hand on the walker, the other on the carriage seat.

"Allow me, *signora*." The guy with the gold earrings hurried around the carriage. "I'm Gino, and I will make sure you have the smoothest ride in the park.''

''Thanks, Gino. I'll take care of her.'' Alex moved in beside them. The protective, proprietary feelings stirring inside him came as no surprise. Not that he was happy about them. Protective he understood. He felt that way about the animals he treated. That instinct was basic to him, but the proprietary feeling toward Jenny was not. It was wrong. He had no rights where Jenny was concerned. And he was beginning not to care much for that idea, either.

''How about I take care of this?'' Gino put a hand on the walker.

''Thanks.'' With an arm around her waist, Alex supported Jenny's weight while Gino pulled the walker to the side.

''If you'll just let me lean on you, I think I can lift myself up.'' She set her jaw with determination, but he could see the dampness forming above her lip. The required effort was probably more than she'd anticipated.

''It'll be easier if I lift you up.''

''But I can—''

He bracketed her waist with his hands and gently lifted her high enough to get a foothold. He didn't let go until both feet were planted firmly on the carriage step and she'd grabbed the support rail.

''Okay?'' He kept his hands up, ready to catch her if she fell.

''Okay.'' Her voice sounded a little shaky.

"Here you go." Gino passed her a cushion and a blanket. "It's a little breezy this afternoon."

"Thank you." Jenny placed the cushion on the seat, then arranged the blanket as additional padding.

It was a beautiful late spring day, and the man's thoughtfulness warmed Alex. That taught him for mentally judging the guy by his eyebrow piercing.

"Need anything else?" Gino asked.

"I don't." Jenny looked at Alex.

"You sure you want to do this?"

"Positive."

Alex threw up his hands. "All right. Let's go."

"Don't worry, I'll take it nice and easy," Gino said as he folded up the walker.

"I'd appreciate it." Alex helped him stow the walker on the seat opposite Jenny, then climbed up and realized it probably wouldn't be a good idea to crowd her.

"Here." She patted the seat beside her when he hesitated. "There's plenty of room for both of us."

He didn't have much choice. He eased in slowly, trying not to jostle her. The space was cramped, and he stretched his arm across the seat behind her.

She smiled shyly and snuggled closer, resting her head on his arm. "Thanks, Alex."

"For what?"

"For being you." She looked up at him, her gaze lingering on his mouth, then meeting his eyes.

"Are you two ready?" Gino asked over his shoulder.

It took Alex a moment to register what the man

had said. Jenny's warm sweet breath still seduced his senses. "Ready."

The carriage started to move, and Jenny placed a hand on his chest. She had to feel his heart picking up speed as she tried to find a comfortable position. And if she lowered her hand any farther, he'd have more than his accelerated heart rate to worry about.

"Isn't the park beautiful?" she whispered. "All those brand new leaves. I never knew there were so many shades of green."

Alex smiled. "You grew up in the Berkshire Mountains."

"I know, but I was young and in need of adventure. Believe me, I did not notice the trees or the leaves. That sort of thing didn't impress me then."

The way the sun turned her shiny hair a cinnamon color was of more interest to him at the moment. "And it does now?"

She lifted her head and seemed to deliberately meet his eyes. "Yeah, it does."

"And Cooper's Corner?"

She gave him a look that made his heart slam. "It has a whole new meaning for me."

CHAPTER NINE

JENNY SHIFTED positions, wincing when she moved too quickly. It was getting easier to sit for longer periods of time, and she hoped to trade the walker in for a cane by the end of the week. Physical therapy wasn't so grueling anymore. At least she didn't get out of bed with dread each morning, wondering what kind of torture Olga had planned for her.

She rearranged the pillow she had propped behind her so she could face Alex. He'd finally put down the file he'd received from the clinic by Federal Express an hour ago. "Anything wrong?"

He seemed a little agitated. "A Great Dane I've been treating has stopped responding to his medication, and he's quit eating."

"Sounds serious. What's wrong with him?"

"Cancer."

Jenny wondered how difficult it was for Alex to treat animals with potentially terminal diseases. He was such a compassionate man, so responsible and committed to doing his best for his patients.

From her short stay in Cooper's Corner, Jenny had seen how many people depended on him and how willingly he made himself available to them.

Folks thought nothing of calling at eleven at night about minor problems with their pets that could have easily waited until morning. Yet she'd never heard Alex once complain or be the slightest bit cross with the caller.

When the sixth-grade teacher from Theodore Cooper Elementary called at the last minute to ask him to speak to her class on veterinary practices, he accepted without hesitation and promptly rearranged his schedule.

Alex briefly closed his eyes and pinched the bridge of his nose. "I'll have to go to the library later, so let me know if you need anything while I'm out."

"For research?"

He nodded and stretched his neck. Maybe the couch wasn't working so well for him as a bed. Maybe she should offer to share hers. She was healing well, and there was enough room, and of course it would be strictly platonic anyway. And maybe...

Damn, she needed to forget that idea. "What about the Internet? You can use my laptop."

His lips curved in a lazy smile. "Call me old-fashioned, but when it comes to my practice, I want a thick sturdy medical book in my hands."

She'd like to put something else in those large capable hands.

Jenny started at the shockingly erotic thought. Her cheeks automatically heated, and if it wouldn't make her look like a total idiot, she'd hightail it to her room in her walker before she said or did something really, really foolish.

"What about Tuck?" That was a stupid question. "I mean, obviously he's worried or he wouldn't be calling you, but isn't he supposed to be taking your cases?"

"Tuck knows more about horses and cattle. He's a trained vet but he's primarily a rancher and hadn't practiced medicine outside his ranch until he moved to Cooper's Corner last Christmas."

"Oh. I thought he'd been here awhile. You seem like such good friends."

"We hit it off right away or else I wouldn't have taken him on as a partner."

"Tell me if I'm being too nosy, but I'm curious. Why did you want a partner?"

Alex shrugged. "It's hard to get away when you're the only vet in town."

She drew her head back in surprise. She'd learned a lot about Alex in the past few weeks. He was a homebody and might even be semi-reclusive if not for his job. "I didn't realize you took a lot of time off."

"I don't. That's the point. But I figured it would be nice to do some traveling."

"Oh." That piece of news did more than surprise her—it shocked her. "Where would you like to travel?

He lifted a shoulder. "Wherever the spirit moves me."

This didn't sound at all like Alex. "You never said anything."

He lifted a brow.

"I didn't mean that you owe me an explanation or anything, it's just that now you've been burdened with me, and—"

"Hey, stop." He caught and held her gaze. "You're not a burden."

"Yeah, but—"

"Jenny, I'm right where I want to be. The end. No discussion necessary."

Yet another side to Alex. He wasn't usually so stern. "I still have a lot of contacts in the hotel industry. I can probably get you some good room rates when you're ready."

"Great," he said with a definite lack of enthusiasm.

She wasn't feeling so chipper herself. It was ridiculous for her to feel this unsettled to learn he had a serious case of wanderlust. Was it caused by guilt, knowing he couldn't go anywhere for another eight months or so because of her?

Or maybe she felt a little bereft at the thought of Alex leaving Cooper's Corner, even for a vacation. Whenever she thought of settling there, she pictured Alex being there as a friend. She watched him gather his paperwork, drawn by his long, lean fingers, and her stomach tensed. Who was she kidding? She hadn't thought of Alex as merely a friend in almost a month.

But that's apparently all he wanted to be to her. She didn't doubt there was some physical attraction. He'd subtly expressed interest from time to time, but obviously not enough to act on beyond a few kisses.

"Have you thought about what you want for lunch?" he asked, briefly glancing at her before tucking the file into the envelope.

"A hot fudge sundae."

His gaze flew up again, his eyes narrowed. "Seriously?"

She gave him a solemn nod. "Very seriously."

"You must be feeling better."

"I told you I have been. Within the next three days, Dr. Sage should give me the okay to go home. Now, about that hot fudge sundae…"

A slight frown drew Alex's brows together, and he studied her with unnerving intensity. "Home meaning Cooper's Corner or our house?"

"Is there a right answer?" she joked, but he didn't smile. How was she supposed to answer a question like that? "Both, I guess." She moistened her lips and quickly added, "I know it's only temporary, but I do consider your house home. But just for now."

"It is your home."

"And the farm." She hurried on, hoping she hadn't said anything that put her foot in it. "It's great that Tuck's taken over Dad's chickens, but I'm going to have to start thinking about what to do with the house. Obviously I can't afford to fix it up."

"Would you want to?"

She shrugged, curious to see his puzzled expression. "It's a moot point."

"Humor me. If you had the money, would you fix it up?"

"It's not that simple."

GET 2

HOW TO GET YOUR
2 FREE BOOKS AND FREE GIFT!

1. Peel off the MIRA® sticker on the front cover. Place it in the space provided at right. This automatically entitles you to receive two free books and an exciting surprise gift.

2. Send back this card and you'll get 2 "The Best of the Best™" books. These books have a combined cover price of $11.98 or more in the U.S. and $13.98 or more in Canada, but they are yours to keep absolutely FREE!

3. There's <u>no</u> catch. You're under <u>no</u> obligation to buy anything. We charge nothing – ZERO – for your first shipment. And you don't have to make any minimum number of purchases – not even one!

4. We call this line "The Best of the Best" because each month you'll receive the best books by some of today's most popular authors. These authors show up time and time again on all the major bestseller lists and their books sell out as soon as they hit the stores. You'll like the convenience of getting them delivered to your home at our special discount prices . . . and you'll love your *Heart to Heart* subscriber newsletter featuring author news, horoscopes, recipes, book reviews and much more!

5. We hope that after receiving your free books you'll want to remain a subscriber. But the choice is yours – to continue or cancel, anytime at all! So why not take us up on our invitation, with no risk of any kind. You'll be glad you did!

6. And remember...we'll send you a surprise gift ABSOLUTELY FREE just for giving THE BEST OF THE BEST a try.

SPECIAL FREE GIFT!
We'll send you a fabulous surprise gift, absolutely FREE, simply for accepting our no-risk offer!

Visit us online at
www.mirabooks.com

BOOKS FREE!

Hurry!

Return this card promptly to GET 2 FREE BOOKS & A FREE GIFT!

YES! Please send me the 2 FREE "The Best of the Best" books and FREE gift for which I qualify. I understand that I am under no obligation to purchase anything further, as explained on the back and on the opposite page.

Affix peel-off MIRA sticker here

385 MDL DRTA   185 MDL DR59

FIRST NAME	LAST NAME

ADDRESS

APT.#	CITY

STATE/PROV.	ZIP/POSTAL CODE

THE BEST OF THE BEST™ — Here's How it Works:

Accepting your 2 free books and gift places you under no obligation to buy anything. You may keep the books and gift and return the shipping statement marked "cancel." If you do not cancel, about a month later we will send you 4 additional books and bill you just $4.74 each in the U.S., or $5.24 each in Canada, plus 25¢ shipping & handling per book and applicable taxes if any.* That's the complete price and — compared to cover prices starting from $5.99 each in the U.S. and $6.99 each in Canada — it's quite a bargain! You may cancel at any time, but if you choose to continue, every month we'll send you 4 more books, which you may either purchase at the discount price or return to us and cancel your subscription.

*Terms and prices subject to change without notice. Sales tax applicable in N.Y. Canadian residents will be charged applicable provincial taxes and GST. Credit or Debit balances in a customer's account(s) may be offset by any other outstanding balance owed by or to the customer.

A flash of disappointment in his eyes made her even more curious. "Because that would mean you'd have to stick around Cooper's Corner."

"That isn't it at all." She didn't know what he was getting at, but she didn't like being questioned. Especially since the truth might scare the hell out of him, and she didn't want to do that.

"Yeah? So what is it?"

"Why do you want to know?"

He looked hurt. "Why wouldn't I be curious? The land borders mine."

So his interest wasn't personal. Not anything to do with her, anyway. She should have been relieved. "I'd love to be able to keep the place. The farm has been in the Taylor family for generations. But how could I make a living? I don't know how to farm. My father did, and he couldn't even make a go of it."

"Your father didn't have his heart in it."

"What do you mean? He loved the place. And he did have some small success with his chickens."

"Never mind." Alex pushed a hand through his hair and got up. "This conversation is pointless."

"Wait a minute. I want to know about my father."

"Thought of anything you need while I'm at the library? I might as well head out so I can be back before rush hour."

"Damn it, Alex, don't you dare walk out in the middle of this."

"Middle of what? I asked if you wanted to keep the farm, and you said you didn't. That's it."

"Don't put words in my mouth. And don't try and change the subject, either."

He grabbed the keys off the counter. She couldn't believe it. He was going to leave without finishing their discussion. She tried to struggle to her feet, but in her haste she kept slipping.

"Don't do that, Jen." Alex was beside her in a moment with a steadying hand, his voice low and soothing. "I'm not going anywhere yet."

She wanted to cry. She felt so helpless suddenly. And on top of everything, she'd bumped the incision and now she hurt. "Damn it, damn it, damn it."

He sat next to her on the couch, his lips curving in a faint smile.

"Don't look at me like that."

He brushed a strand of hair out of her eyes. "Like what?"

"Like 'I told you so.'"

He shook his head. "Are you all right?"

"Of course." She swallowed, more embarrassed than in pain. "I know I wasn't the daughter he wanted."

He reared his head back in genuine surprise. "You can't believe that. He was so proud of you."

"I know, but still, he wanted me to— I left him. He had no one. It had always been just the two of us. He was both mother and father to me, and I left him."

"Jen, don't." Alex put an arm around her shoulders and hugged her. "Do you think he expected you to stick around? How much opportunity is there for a bright, ambitious young woman in Cooper's Corner?''

She sniffed. Alex was being kind, but none of that mattered. She'd left her father alone, and the guilt nagged at her.

"How many of your friends from high school still live there?''

"Only one, but that's not the point."

"You think your father would have wanted you to stay just so he wouldn't be alone? Would he have wanted you to forgo a career in which you obviously have done very well?''

"You don't understand."

"More than you think. Your dad missed you, of course, but he wasn't lonely. Several times a week we had dinner together and played a couple of games of chess. He regularly delivered fresh eggs and chickens to Maureen at the B and B and usually ended up staying for breakfast and fixing a few things around the place for her. They got to be pretty good friends.

"Every other Saturday evening he and a few others played cards at Philo and Phyllis's house. He volunteered for the annual Fourth of July picnic and the Founders Day barbecue. Don't think he shut himself in because you were gone."

"You're not making me feel much better," she muttered. Why hadn't she known all this? Of course her father had told her about some of his activities. Had she been so self-absorbed for the past few years that their letters and conversations had all revolved around her? "I should have known more about him, about what he did every day—"

"Jen." He squeezed her shoulders. "He lived on a farm. His life was pretty routine most of the time. Raising chickens and playing cards on Saturday nights isn't much to talk about."

She sighed. Some of what he said made sense, but still he didn't understand what it was like growing up without a mother and having your father play both roles. Ed had sacrificed for her many times, and she'd skipped town.

"Don't look for ways to feel guilty and beat yourself up. That's a familiar and comfortable emotion so our minds immediately go there. But it's destructive thinking, a no-win situation."

"You know this from experience?" she asked, instantly regretting her defensive attack.

He didn't even blink. "Yes."

Jenny looked away. "I guess we've all experienced guilt, whether justified or not."

"That we can agree on."

At the quiet humor in his voice, she met his eyes again. He gave her a reassuring smile, and she gathered her courage and asked, "Do you have regrets about Sara? I mean, do you still think about her a lot?"

He flinched, and she heard his sharp intake of breath.

Jenny shrunk away from him. "Forget it. That was too personal. I'm sorry."

"That's all right. You just caught me off guard."

"Still, we don't have to talk about it. Really."

"It's okay, Jen. Really."

His imitation of her was perfect, and she made a face at him.

Alex smiled. "Yeah, I still think about Sara. Mostly when something reminds me of her and triggers a memory. But I don't think about her every day like I did when she died. Then my thoughts were almost obsessive, crippling. I had trouble going to work. Good thing I was the only vet in town at the time because it forced me into the mainstream."

"I remember her only vaguely. Didn't her family move into town when she was in high school?"

He nodded. "I was a senior and she was in the ninth grade, but she'd come from a gifted program in Boston, and we were assigned a science project together."

"I bet that hurt your tender male ego," Jenny teased, sensing that he wasn't upset by the conversation.

"Damn right. I was seventeen, a jock and top of the class, while she was only in the ninth grade and a *girl.*"

Jenny laughed. "Poor Sara. She didn't know what she was in for."

"Poor Sara nothing. The first thing she told me was that whatever macho crap I was feeling, to get over it."

"We would have been great friends."

He became serious, and Jenny was suddenly afraid she'd said too much.

"You do remind me of her in some ways," Alex said at last. "Like her, you're a strong, independent woman who knows what you want."

Jenny started to say something then closed her mouth. She didn't want to open herself up to questions. Until this past month, she'd thought of herself in precisely that way, but now she was so damned confused she didn't know what to think.

The notion of staying in Cooper's Corner had taken a hold on her she didn't understand. Of course, part of it had to do with Alex. She could hardly spend all this time with him and not get attached.

But what would she do for a living if she did stay? And how would Alex feel about her living in the same town once she was on her feet and they got a divorce? Would he feel threatened? Would he think she was cramping his style?

"What's going on in that pretty head of yours? You look awfully melancholy."

"What?" Jenny realized she'd been off in her own world too long. She shrugged. "No, I was just thinking about the comment I made about Sara and me being friends, and that got me wondering about the age difference between us. I had to be in grade school when she arrived in Cooper's Corner. That's why I don't remember her too well."

"Ah, small town life. Everyone knows when everyone else comes and goes. Sure you don't miss it?"

"That part? Definitely not."

They both chuckled.

Comfortably relaxed with his arm around her shoulder, she decided to push her luck. "Can I be nosy and ask one more question?"

"Shoot."

"Why didn't you have kids?"

Immediately he tensed. "We'd planned on starting a family." He paused. "We disagreed on when to start, and then it was too late."

God, when was she going to learn to leave well enough alone? She shouldn't have asked something so personal. And she definitely wouldn't ask who wanted to wait, even though she was crazy to know.

"You asked if I had any regrets. That would be the biggest one I have. Waiting to have children."

She put her hand over his. It was so much larger than hers, she barely covered any of it. He turned his hand over so that their palms met. "Remember, don't beat yourself up over it. You probably wanted to get established in your practice and get the clinic off the ground. That's perfectly understandable."

"I'm not the one who wanted to wait."

"Sara did?" Jenny mentally shook her head at the inane remark. "I don't know why I made the assumption it was you."

"It doesn't matter. The end result is the same."

She squeezed his hand, and his lips curved into a sad smile. She hated seeing him look like this. Why the heck had she brought up the subject? "You can still have children."

One brow lifted in amusement. "Are you offering?"

Jenny started to sputter a response, but Alex quickly intervened.

"Don't worry. It was just a joke."

She coughed to buy herself time to calm down.

"Are you okay? Lean forward and let me tap you on the back."

She shook her head. "I'm fine. I knew you were joking. You just took me by surprise."

"You okay now?"

"Fine." Except her mood had gone south. "I only meant that if children are important to you, it's not too late."

"You're right. But it takes two, remember?"

"Oh, really? Gee, I'd forgotten."

Her sarcasm got a smile out of him. "Like I said before, I'm old-fashioned. I want to be married to my children's mother."

"But you said you'd never get married again." Jiminy Christmas, why couldn't she let the matter drop?

"Yes, I did." He looked as if he wanted to say more but fell silent, studying her as if searching for some kind of cue.

Did he want her to push for an answer? Was she standing in his way? He'd assured her otherwise. Nothing had changed in the two months they'd been married.

Except maybe their relationship.

She moistened her lips before saying, "I've always wanted children, too."

"Yeah?" Something sparked in his eyes, some indefinable emotion that started her heart pumping faster. "What's stopped you?"

"I guess I'm old-fashioned, too. I haven't found the right guy yet."

"You must have met a lot of men in your line of work."

"Yup, but no one that got me thinking long term." She exhaled slowly, hoping to steady her pulse. Alex got her thinking long term. There was no point denying it. Maybe it was because she was vulnerable. Maybe the feeling would eventually pass. She had no idea. But right this minute she'd crawl into bed with him if he asked.

He glanced at his watch, and disappointment surged through her. He was probably more concerned about getting to the library. And he should be. The research was important. She wished he'd ask more questions about her goals as far as a family. Maybe they were more compatible than he thought.

Maybe she ought to give him a deep, wet kiss that would let him know she wanted more than friendship. Oh, God, she hated this stuff.

When he stretched his neck again and winced, she decided to seize the opportunity. "This couch isn't working out for you, is it?"

"For another two or three days it'll be just fine."

She held her breath. "I have a queen-size bed. I know it would be a little short, but it's still longer than the couch."

He frowned and shook his head. "No way are you sleeping out here."

"I wasn't suggesting that."

His eyes met hers, and she knew darn well she didn't imagine the flicker of desire she saw in them.

"Like I said…" She cleared her throat. "It's a big bed. Big enough for both of us."

"I don't know, Jen…" He rubbed his jaw, looking agitated.

At any moment, she was going to die of mortification. Not because she was about to get rejected but that she'd been stupid enough to ask in the first place.

"It's tempting." He stared her in the eyes. The pulse at his throat leaped like crazy. "But I'm so afraid of hurting you. I may roll over in my sleep and press against your back and… I don't know."

A nervous giggle escaped her when she realized it was her physical well-being he was concerned with.

He frowned. "What is it?"

"You won't hurt me. I promise. The incision is so well padded. We can even sleep with a couple of pillows between us if it'll make you feel better."

The shadow of disappointment that crossed his face made her heart soar. "There are other reasons it might not be a good idea."

"Such as?" Made brave by his reaction, she leaned closer so that their breath mingled.

His gaze dropped to her lips, and he moved closer. They'd barely made contact when someone knocked at the door.

She jerked back. No one knocked at her door. Ever. Hardly ever, anyway. And certainly not before they were buzzed into the building.

"Who's that?" Alex got up.

"I have no idea."

He looked through the peephole. "It's a man…late twenties, early thirties."

"Tall? Dark hair? Blue eyes?"

"Dark hair. I don't know about the eyes."

Was it Steven? Was he back in town? He lived two doors down. He wouldn't need to be buzzed in. "I think I know who it is." Excited to see her friend, she motioned to Alex to open the door. "Go ahead and let him in."

Alex unlocked the dead bolt and opened the door. Steven stood in the doorway. He gave Alex a curious look and stepped back, but when he saw Jenny, he broke into a big smile.

"Honey, where have you been?" he cried, rushing over to kiss her.

CHAPTER TEN

"I THOUGHT you were still in Paris."

"I got in last night. Brian told me you'd called last week, and I came right over."

Alex shouldn't have been annoyed. It was none of his business whom Jenny called—or that the guy was extraordinarily good-looking and sitting so close to Jenny he was practically on her lap.

"Oh, gosh, I'm sorry." Jenny smiled at Alex. "This is my very good friend, Steven Casper." She leaned into him when he put his arm around her. "Steven, this is Alex McAlester."

It didn't escape Alex's notice that she didn't refer to him as her husband. Or friend.

Steven got up and extended his hand. The guy had a smile that probably had women lining up to do his laundry. "Good to meet you, Alex."

"Same here. Please, sit." *Just not next to Jenny.*

Steven resumed his position beside Jenny, his arm around her shoulders. "You look a little pale. Are you okay?"

"Fine." She smiled and squeezed his thigh. "Happy to see you."

Alex figured he ought to ask the guy if he would

like something to drink, except he didn't really want him sticking around. Instead, he took a seat opposite them in an uncomfortable thrift shop armchair.

He wondered why Jenny had never mentioned Steven. The guy seemed awfully familiar with her, though it didn't appear she'd told him about the surgery.

"I'm so sorry I couldn't be with you for your father's funeral, honey." Steven twirled a strand of Jenny's hair around his finger. "I was in Rome, and I couldn't get to Boston and back in time. How did it go?"

She shrugged, the mention of the funeral bringing sadness to her eyes. "As well as could be expected, I guess. He had so many friends who attended." She smiled at Alex with a fondness that tightened his chest. "Really good friends."

Steven looked at Alex with new interest. "Are you from Cooper's Town?"

"Cooper's Corner," Jen and Alex said at the same time.

"I stand corrected." Steven laughed and turned his attention to Jenny without waiting for an answer. "I went to that restaurant in Florence that you recommended, and it was fabulous."

"Thank goodness. I haven't been there for three years. I was hoping it hadn't gone downhill. What about the Musé d'Orsay in Paris? Did you make it there?"

Steven shook his head. "I didn't have time. Maybe next trip."

Alex sat in shock, only vaguely listening as they discussed different European cities and museums and restaurants. When had Jenny gone to Europe? Ed hadn't mentioned anything. And Ed had told him everything Jenny was doing.

He stared at her, feeling as if he was looking at someone he didn't know. She'd thrown him a few nervous glances, which confirmed his suspicion that there were aspects of Jenny's life Ed had known nothing about.

And this guy Steven. How did he fit into the picture? Jenny had never mentioned him, and neither had Ed. He didn't seem to be a boyfriend. He'd know more about Jenny's medical problems if he were. Maybe they had a casual relationship. No-strings-attached sex.

The very thought drove a dagger through Alex's heart. No, he had no rights to her. They had a no-strings-attached relationship, as well. Foolishly he'd started to think they could have more, that perhaps she could enjoy a life in Cooper's Corner. With him. Now he wasn't sure. He wasn't sure of anything.

"So, tell me about you," Steven said, sandwiching her hands between his. "Have you found another job yet?"

"No, but I haven't been looking." She glanced at Alex. "I'm married, Steven. Alex is my husband."

He looked at Alex in surprise, and then his gaze went to Jenny. "You little devil. You never breathed a word about another man in your life." Grinning, he leaned over and kissed her lightly on the lips. He didn't let go of her hands, either. Pretty nervy considering what she'd just told him. "Congratulations. To both of you."

"Thanks," Alex mumbled, twice as confused over their relationship. Maybe they were platonic friends. No matter, there was still a lot about Jenny that Alex apparently didn't know, and it ate at him.

"So, you're going to live here, I hope?" Steven asked pleasantly.

She shook her head. "Actually, I've given up the apartment and we'll be heading to Cooper's Corner in a few days."

"Oh, no. I'll miss you. Who can I bitch to when the super tells me the squeak in our plumbing is all in my head?"

Jenny laughed. "You've never had trouble finding someone to bitch to."

Steven placed a dramatic hand on his chest. "You wound me."

She gave Alex an apologetic look. "You're probably wondering what in the heck we're talking about. Steven is my neighbor from two doors down. He and the building superintendent have not gotten along from day one."

"No one gets along with that arrogant SOB." Steven waved a hand. "Anyway, I can't believe you're leaving the city, the bright lights, the fast pace. Honey, you're going to miss it, and then just try finding another rent-controlled apartment when you come crawling back."

Jenny smiled. "I could always stay in your apartment. You're never there."

"True. In fact, I fly back to Rome in two weeks for a Versace show."

"Steven's a model," she told Alex. "You've probably seen him in ads for Ralph Lauren."

A model. That made sense. The perfect hair, perfect teeth, perfect smile. He was also too self-absorbed to realize Alex had never seen him in an ad or heard of him before. In fact, he barely acknowledged Alex and kept talking to Jenny, who slipped Alex odd glances.

"Brian and I would love to take you two to dinner in celebration of your wedding." Steven looked at Alex then. "You name the night and restaurant. I'll make the reservations."

"Unfortunately, I don't think we'll have time." Alex tried to appear apologetic as he met Jenny's eyes.

In spite of her skeptical look, she said, "You're right. We have too much to do before we leave."

Alex found it strange that she never mentioned the surgery. Nor did Steven ask about her health. They couldn't be *that* good friends if he didn't know she'd been in great pain for more than a year. Petty, Alex knew, but the thought appealed greatly to him.

"How about I bring over lunch then?" Steven scanned the room. "Do you need help packing? I could order something from Fazzio's to be delivered, and we could pack and catch up on what's been happening at the same time."

"I don't know." Jenny looked confused. "Alex? What do you think?"

"That's your call, sweetheart."

At the endearment, her eyebrows rose. "You may need some help with the lifting."

Steven bent his elbow to show off a muscular bicep. "I'm all yours. Use and abuse me."

Jenny laughed and shook her head. "Knock it off, Steven."

He grinned and winked.

Obviously it was a private joke between them that Alex didn't get. But he liked the fact that Steven seemed sincere about helping with the manual labor. Out of jealousy, maybe Alex had misjudged him. The thought he was capable of jealousy chafed.

"Thanks, but I've arranged for professional movers to pack up. Jenny just needs to decide what she's taking and what she wants to get rid of."

She gave him a dark look Steven caught, judging by the speculative frown he bounced between them.

What the hell had he done to deserve that look? Alex wondered.

"I'll start sorting through things after you leave for the library," she said, her tone a little cool. "What day are the movers coming?"

"Either Thursday or Friday, depending when you get—" He stopped himself just in time. He'd almost blown it and mentioned needing the doctor to release her to travel. If she'd wanted her friend to know about the surgery, she would have told him by now.

No one said anything, and then Steven stood. "I think I forgot a cake in the oven."

Jenny sighed and gave him a dry look.

Steven chuckled. "You guys apparently need to do some talking. I'll buzz you later."

Almost as if on cue, Alex's cell phone rang. He answered it, knowing it had to be Tuck. It was. Their conversation was brief. The news wasn't good. Within a minute he disconnected the call.

"I have to fly to Boston right away," he told Jenny. "There'll be a car waiting to take me to Cooper's Corner."

"Is it the Great Dane?"

He nodded grimly.

"Go get your things. I'll call the airline."

"I'm sorry, Jen. I'll try my best to get back by tomorrow night."

"Do whatever you have to do. Don't worry about me. I'll be fine."

"I'll look after her," Steven said, appearing totally confused.

Alex shook the guy's hand. "Thanks," he said with very mixed emotions.

JENNY WISHED she'd asked Alex to leave her his cell phone. She had the phone in the apartment disconnected as soon as she married Alex and knew she'd be in Cooper's Corner awhile. Now she had no way of reaching him unless she hobbled to the phone booth at the corner. But first she'd have to make it to

Moe's convenience store at the opposite corner to buy a long distance calling card.

Or she could ask Steven if she could use his phone. But she knew he and Brian were gone for the evening because they'd asked her to go out to dinner and then a movie with them. Besides, she'd have no privacy talking to Alex in Steven's apartment, and her friend would have more questions and opinions than a conservative Republican.

She'd known Steven for three years and they had bonded quickly over a couple of skim milk lattés and a discussion regarding tenant's rights when their building elevator had been down for two days.

He was funny and charming and the best-looking guy she'd ever met. When she'd discovered he was gay and that Brian was his partner of six years, she'd been disappointed. But not for long. The easy friendship that had grown between them had become invaluable in some of her darker moments.

She looked at the glowing red numbers of the digital clock and then at her walker and sighed. She might as well get her act together and hoof it to the corner before it got too late. Or should she wait for morning? No, she had to know he got there safely or she wouldn't sleep.

By the time she took a swipe at her hair with a brush and grabbed her keys, someone knocked at the door. She peered through the peephole. It was Steven.

She opened the door. "I thought you went to dinner and a movie."

"Just dinner. I skipped the movie." He strode in past her. "I couldn't wait to get a hold of you alone."

"Why am I not surprised?" There was no getting around it. He'd seen her sitting, and he'd seen her standing. Now he was going to see her hobble. And have a million questions.

He folded his arms across his chest. "I want to know what you're hiding."

Apparently he hadn't seen the folded walker resting against the wall behind the door or the cane she used around the apartment. Leaning on the cane, she took her first shaky step.

He watched her a moment, then asked bluntly, "What happened?"

She'd known better than to think she could avoid telling him the whole sordid story. But at least she didn't have to do it in front of Alex. "I had surgery almost three weeks ago."

"Those stupid quacks finally found out what was wrong." Steven's disdain for doctors was no secret. "Come sit down."

He started to take her arm, but she gently stopped him. "It's better if I go at my own pace."

"Sure." He stood back and waited for her to settle on the couch, propped against the cushions she kept carefully arranged there. "Okay? Can I get you anything?"

"A stiff drink maybe?"

He frowned. "Aren't you taking medication?"

"I'm kidding. Just sit."

"Now, what's going on?" He sat beside her,

though not too close, and was careful not to jostle the cushions. "Honey, you have one hell of a lot to tell me. I can't believe you got married. Who is he?"

"You're more concerned about Alex than the surgery?"

"Damn right. You're already recovering from the surgery, aren't you?"

"The implication being?"

"Marriage can be a lasting thorn in your side."

Jenny snorted. "This coming from someone who's been with the same person for six years? Are you telling me you're tired of Brian?"

"Of course not. We'll be using each other's rockers and denture cream."

"Thank you for making my point."

"We've known each other for twelve years. How long have you known Alex?"

"Half my life." That was the truth, even though it wasn't quite what Steven meant. She remembered the time in high school when her friend Mandy Wilson had had a crush on Alex.

He'd just graduated from veterinarian school and had gone to Cooper's Corner to set up a clinic. He was ten years older than Mandy and of course didn't give her a second look no matter how many times she took the poor family cat in to see him.

And then Alex had gotten married, and Mandy fell in love with Tim Bergstrom, the guy who managed the Burger Barn. Funny, Jenny had forgotten about all that until now. She couldn't recall much of what she'd thought of Alex, except that he scored major points by being tall and a college boy and having his own car—all impressive credentials to high school sophomore girls.

"Hey, you, let me in on the joke."

She looked at Steven and realized she was grinning. "I was just thinking about a friend who had a crush on Alex when we were in high school."

"He went to high school with you?"

"No, he's ten years older. My friend and I were in high school, and he was already setting up his vet practice."

"Okay, good. The guy's established, at least. What else should I know about him?"

Jenny laughed. "Oh, so now he meets with your approval?"

"Don't get ahead of yourself. Why haven't I heard his name before today?"

That sobered her. Steven had been the closest friend she'd had for the past three years. Why couldn't she tell him the truth, that it wasn't a real marriage? Why should she care if he knew? It wasn't as if he'd run to the insurance company and cry fraud.

No, her reluctance stemmed from something much more personal. Even more personal than protecting her privacy.

She wanted to pretend they had a real marriage, to let the world think this was happily ever after. She wanted Alex to start seeing her as a wife, not as a stray he'd rescued.

When she'd joined her therapy group and was having a difficult time being optimistic, someone advised her to "fake it till you make it." She hadn't gotten it at first. She thought the person was a lunatic with rose-colored glasses. But as time and healing progressed, she understood the concept and hung on to it for all she was worth.

That's how she was going to treat Alex from now on, she decided—as if she were his real wife. If Alex didn't like it, he'd have to tell her.

"Why do I get the feeling that you haven't listened to a word I've said?"

She grinned. "How astute of you."

"What? Marriage has made you sarcastic?"

"And sassy and happy."

Steven smiled. "You do look happy, and I guess that's all I should care about. It just seems so damn sudden."

"Not really. You've been going back and forth to Europe so much lately that we haven't talked for more than ten minutes at a time."

"Tell me about it. Brian is getting on my case. He wants me to take two months off after this next show. My agent would kill me."

Jenny squeezed his hand. "Brian is right. You've been pushing hard. Life's too short to spend it at work."

"Poor kid, you've learned the hard way." Steven shook his head. "I still think you should sue the bastards for firing you when you were sick."

"I couldn't perform my job. They needed someone who could." She lifted a silencing hand when he looked ready to argue. "I can't afford the negative energy, okay?"

He gave her a grudging nod. "So tell me, what did the quacks finally find out?"

"It was a tumor at the base of my spine."

"Benign, right?"

She nodded.

He sighed, then shook his head. "Damn. First they thought it was MS and then ALS, and it turns out to be a tumor. And you wonder why I call them quacks."

Jenny sighed. "It was more complicated because of where the tumor was positioned. But I really don't want to get into it."

"No problem. You know me and medical terms...in one ear and out the other. Anyway, I'd rather hear about Alex." He grinned, and she groaned. "But first I think I'll make some tea. Want some?"

"Sure." Maybe she'd luck out and he'd think of something else to tell her about his trip. She didn't want to discuss Alex because she'd very likely say something she shouldn't.

Steven had just gotten to the kitchen when his cell phone rang. He turned and stared blankly at her.

"Aren't you going to answer it?"

"It's not mine." He patted his pocket. "I don't even have it with me. It sounds like it's coming from your room."

"Alex must have left the phone." She started to

jump up and winced when her foolishness dealt her a sharp pain.

"Stay right there. I've got it." Steven disappeared into her room and she heard him answer the call as he walked back. "Just a minute." He held out the phone. "It's your hubby."

She couldn't help the grin that broke out on her face and the way her heart leaped as she took the phone. "Hi, honey."

Alex paused. "Hi. I'm here at the clinic. What's Steven doing there? He better not be moving in on you while I'm gone."

"Of course not." Hadn't he figured out Steven was gay by now? She had to admit that the thought he might be a little jealous pleased her.

Alex chuckled. "I'm teasing. I'm glad you have the company. Everything okay?"

"Fine. How's the dog doing?"

"Not good." His voice sounded grim. "I may have to take him to a facility in Boston. I won't know until later tonight."

"Oh, Alex, I'm sorry. The owner must be a wreck."

"Yeah, but we'll do all we can and pray for the best."

"Whatever happens, don't worry about me. I'm absolutely fine. I promise."

"I'll always worry about you, Jen," he said softly. "I've gotta go. Sleep well."

"You, too."

"I'll call you tomorrow morning."

She had the sudden urge to tell Alex she loved him. Wouldn't Steven expect her to say something like that to her husband? Heck, it had nothing to do with Steven listening. She did love Alex, and she wanted him to know.

"I love you," she whispered, just as she heard the call disconnect.

ALEX REPLACED the receiver and stared at the phone. He'd seen her less than five hours ago. How could he miss her this much already? It was ridiculous. Of course they'd spent nearly every waking hour together for the past two weeks, and the week before that he'd spent visiting her for hours in the hospital.

Yet how well did he really know her? Hearing her discuss cities in Europe with Steven had unnerved Alex. It was almost as if she'd had a secret life her father didn't know about, except she didn't seem at all hesitant to talk about her travels in front of Alex.

He'd have to ask her about it once he got back to New York. The explanation was probably simple, the travel work-related. But not knowing would eat at him.

"I've got Zeus stabilized." Tuck walked into Alex's office, pulling off his gloves. "We should know something by the end of the night. If we need to transport him to Boston, everything is ready on that end."

Alex nodded. "His age concerns me, otherwise I'd do the surgery here."

Tuck gave him a sympathetic smile. ''I wouldn't want to be in your shoes, buddy. But for what it's worth, I think you're doing the right thing.''

''I hope so.'' He stared at the dog's chart. Zeus had to be okay. Jenny had to make a full recovery. He turned from Tuck, his face suddenly warm, his chest tight. Hadn't he learned anything after Sara? People didn't always get better. People died. Loving them wasn't enough.

CHAPTER ELEVEN

"HELLO, Jenny, hello!"

Jenny tried to ignore Plato and concentrate on doing her leg lifts. It was bad enough the simple exercise seemed grueling at times and often hurt. She sure didn't need Plato's two cents.

"Push harder, Jenny."

"Darn it. Would you please keep your big beak shut for two minutes?"

"Darn it, Jenny."

She growled in frustration at the stubborn bird, and he squawked back. That did it. One of them had to go. And since she needed the open space of the living room to do her daily exercises, it was Plato who'd get booted out.

"Don't stop, Jenny."

"You stop it. Right now. Or I'm going to make soup out of you, got it?"

A deep chuckle came from behind.

"Hello, Alex, hello!"

Jenny hung on to the back of the chair for support and turned. "You're home early."

"I'm beat." He smiled and rubbed his eyes. "We have only one overnight boarder that my assistant, Heather, is tending to. How are the exercises going?"

"The exercises are fine. It's my blood pressure that's sky-high."

"Plato's annoying you."

"He's taken over your job of bullying me."

"I don't bully you."

She gave him a dry look and, mimicking him, said, "'Jenny, have you done your exercises today? I bet you can do another set. Push harder—'"

"Push harder, Jenny." Plato had his beak up to the wire of the cage, watching the action.

"See what I mean?" She groaned and gave the bird a dirty look. "How would you like me to drape your cage for the next week?"

Alex laughed. "You realize you're arguing with a bird."

"And losing. How pathetic is that?"

"Pretty bad." He rubbed the back of his neck then stretched it to the side. "You want me to move him?"

Jenny looked at Plato, who was staring at her. The idea of not having him squawk at her all day suddenly seemed unappealing. Even when she passed the living room on her way to the kitchen, he hollered out her name and made her laugh. He really wasn't bad company. "No, it's all right. Leave him there."

Alex grinned and headed toward the sofa. "Okay."

"What?" She sniffed. "Don't get the wrong impression that he's starting to grow on me."

"Of course not."

"I just don't want to disrupt his routine. After all, it is his home."

"It's your home, too, Jen." Alex's amusement faded. "You do feel comfortable here, don't you?"

"Yes, you've been wonderful."

For whatever reason, he didn't seem pleased at that declaration.

"Before you sit down," she said quickly, "would you mind helping me over to the sofa? Plato's been working me hard, and I need to conserve my energy."

At the sound of his name, Plato said, "Hello, Jenny, hello."

She sighed. "Okay, I think the next bird you bring home should be a canary or something. They don't know how to talk, right?"

He slipped an arm around her waist, and his expression lightened. "No more birds unless you approve of them first. How's that?"

"I was only kidding." Even if she weren't, how would she be able to deny him anything when he was this close, his warm breath tickling her ear?

She didn't really need help getting to the sofa. Occasionally she'd ask him just to feel his arm around her, to bring him within kissing distance, but then she'd chicken out.

They'd been home from New York for over a week, and the distance Alex kept between them made her a little crazy. She understood that he'd neglected the clinic for the three weeks he'd spent with her in New York and had a lot to catch up on. She felt bad about that and knew she was being selfish, but she missed his attention.

And she couldn't help wondering how much time

he really needed to spend at work. Or was he trying to stay away from her? Maybe there had been too much togetherness in New York. Maybe he'd learned some things about her he didn't like.

"You seem to be favoring your left leg." He guided her to the sofa and waited until she lowered herself onto it. "Is that normal?"

The genuine concern in his eyes warmed her. "I think I usually end up favoring my right one and then I wear it out and alternate."

"What does the physical therapist say about that?"

Jenny shrugged. "Not to do it."

Alex's mouth curved in a faint smile, and he shook his head. "I'm glad you're such a good patient."

"I am. Don't you think I've progressed well?"

"I think you're on your feet too much."

"The doctor says that as long as I'm not in pain, it's okay."

"But you've often experienced pain or had problems balancing in the past week."

"Not really."

He gave her a sympathetic smile coated with condescension. "Yes, you have, like a moment ago when you had to ask me for help."

She sighed. She would probably be sorry, but... "I wasn't in pain or off balance. I was trying to get you to touch me."

Alarm flickered in his face. "I see."

"No, you don't."

"You're right," he murmured, looking endearing and uncertain.

She sighed again and laid her head back, her eyes closed. "Never mind."

"Jen?"

"Yes?"

She felt him draw closer, and when she opened her eyes, he was right there, his face inches from hers. He touched her lips with his, gently, growing more insistent before he retreated.

"I've wanted to do that for the past month," he whispered.

"So what took you so long?" She slid her arms around his neck and pulled him in for another kiss.

He wasn't so gentle this time. He teased the seam of her lips with his tongue until she opened to him, and his mouth slanted across hers, demanding and purposeful. She couldn't breathe, didn't want to breathe—the only thing she wanted was to make the moment last forever.

All too quickly, he pulled away. His face was dazed and troubled. "God, I hope I didn't hurt you."

"You didn't." She clutched the front of his shirt and drew him toward her.

He didn't resist, but met her eager mouth for another deep, knee-weakening kiss. His large wonderful hands stayed gentle at her waist, and when she ran her palms down his chest to his belt, he moaned softly.

"We have to be careful, Jen."

"Why?"

"I don't want to hurt your back."

She smiled, pleased that's all he meant, that he

wasn't making an emotional withdrawal. "You won't. I promise."

"Neither of us can make that promise." He edged away. "I can't be responsible for injuring you."

"Come on, Alex, we're only kissing." She leaned toward him and brushed his lips with hers.

He mumbled something against her mouth then kissed her hard. It didn't last long. He withdrew, his breathing fast and ragged. "God, Jen, this isn't good—I'm not thinking clearly."

"On the contrary, I think that's very good." She tugged at his shirt again, and he came to her easily with a shadow of self-disgust on his face. "Alex, please don't worry. I'm a big girl and I know what I'm doing."

"Come this way," he said, and reclined slightly, grasping one of her elbows and urging her to follow. The hard thickness under his fly sent a tingle down her spine. "If you lean toward me there'll be no pressure on your lower back."

That he was looking for a way for them to maintain intimacy fueled her excitement, and she did as he asked, pressing against him and feeling his heated length. She moaned softly with pure pleasure.

He stiffened. "Jen, are you okay?"

"More than okay." She unfastened his top two buttons. "Take off your shirt."

He hesitated, doubt warring with desire in his eyes, and then finished freeing the buttons until his shirt hung open. She ran her palms up his chest, over the soft hair and budding nipples. He sank back, and she let her weight rest on him, her breasts pressed to his midriff.

Alex slipped one hand between them and lifted the hem of her T-shirt. She drew back slightly so he could pull the shirt up, then helped him yank it over her head. Thank goodness she had on a relatively new red lace bra that showed off some cleavage instead of one of the ratty old sports bras she often wore around the house.

She doubted it mattered to Alex. Not the way he eagerly undid the front clasp and pushed the cups aside. He stared at her breasts, his chest rising and falling in uneven shudders. Gently he cupped one of her breasts and lightly trailed the pad of his thumb over her nipple. It was already hard and ripe and begging for his touch…for his mouth.

"Are you okay, honey?" he asked, tearing his gaze away from her breasts.

She shook her head, and he froze. "I want you to—" A sudden attack of shyness had her tongue-tied. "I want you to use your mouth."

His lips curved in a sexy smile, then he dipped his head and her nipple disappeared between his lips. He hadn't shaved since early morning, and the rough feel of his chin on her skin added to the incredible sensation of having Alex suckle her. It took all her willpower not to cry out. And when he turned his attention to her other breast, she clutched at his shoulders and closed her eyes, hoping and praying this wasn't a dream.

How many nights had she wanted to slip into his

room, crawl between the sheets with him and lay her head on his chest? Feel those large strong hands run up and down her body?

She whimpered at the way he used his tongue to flick her nipple and she arched her back to increase the intensity of the sensation.

He lifted his head and kissed her briefly on the lips. "Are you okay?"

"I'm fine," she said, frustrated. She appreciated his concern, but geez. "How about I let you know if anything is wrong?"

He smiled at her impatience and kissed her again. "That's a deal."

"Hello, Alex. Hello, Jenny." Plato squawked and frantically flapped his wings as if he were trying to get out of the cage.

She groaned. "I'd forgotten about him."

"Plato, shut up."

Jenny chuckled. She'd never once heard Alex get impatient with the obnoxious macaw.

He looked at her, and his annoyed expression softened. "What's so funny?"

"Shut up, Alex."

"Excuse me, please." Alex got off the couch and headed for the cage.

"Hello, Alex."

"Good night, Plato." He threw the covering over the squawking bird.

Jenny started to laugh but cut herself short when Alex turned to come back to the sofa. His opened shirt and exposed chest made her insides flutter. God, he was beautiful. No spare flesh anywhere. Perfect muscle tone.

She swallowed as he sat beside her, his heated gaze going to her breasts. "Maybe we should stop tormenting Plato and go to my bedroom."

His gaze slowly rose to study her face. "We could," he said hesitantly. "But then we might be asking for more trouble than we're willing to tackle." He trailed the back of his fingers down her cheek.

She didn't want to push or make the situation uncomfortable, but she was tired of holding back. Especially since she'd been getting the feeling all week that he felt the same way. "Are you speaking for me or yourself?"

"Your skin…I've irritated it with my beard." He soothed the edges of her lips with light feathery strokes, then lowered his hand to her breasts.

The skin was red there, too, but she hadn't felt any discomfort. He palmed the weight of her breast then dipped his head to lave the abused area with his tongue.

She sucked in a breath and closed her eyes. He could talk in circles all he wanted, but they'd end up in bed. She was sure of it. The only thing that bothered her was Alex seeing the scar. It was in the most horrid place at the top of her fanny. Not only was it ugly, but the sight of it would probably discourage him from becoming intimate for fear he'd hurt her.

"Ah, Alex, that feels so good." She slid her hand down his chest, over his flat belly to his belt buckle.

He didn't react when she tried to tug the belt free,

and when the buckle wouldn't budge, she lowered her hand to cup his hardness. He filled her palm with heat, and her pulse leaped in anticipation.

"Jenny." Her name came out a hoarse whisper, his breath warm and ragged against her breast.

"Alex, please let's go to the bedroom. I want to make love with—"

A loud rap at the kitchen door startled them both.

"Are you expecting anyone?" he asked.

She shook her head, struggling to pull up her bra straps.

"Do we have to answer?"

Another loud knock. "Yoo-hoo! Where is everyone? I have something for you." Phyllis Cooper's undeniably high-pitched voice came from the kitchen. The door had been unlocked, and she'd obviously let herself in.

They scrambled like guilty teenagers. Jenny clasped her bra, grabbed her T-shirt and pulled it over her head, except the hem rolled up and got caught just under her breasts.

Alex fumbled with the buttons of his shirt.

"Yoo-hoo! Alex? Jenny?" Her voice got closer.

Alex jumped to his feet and waved Jenny to stay put. "Coming, Phyllis."

"Oh, I didn't think anyone was home. I was about to leave your dinner on the counter." She appeared at the entryway to the living room, a large foil-wrapped casserole dish in her hands.

Fortunately Jenny had pulled herself together already. She glanced at Alex. One of the buttons on his shirt was in the wrong hole, causing the untucked shirt to gape, a detail that wasn't missed by Phyllis.

Her eyes widened. "Am I interrupting something?"

"Of course not." Jenny patted her hair, only too aware what a mess it was.

Alex didn't respond, unless she counted the annoyed look on his face.

"I didn't find out until yesterday that you two were back from New York. Been back almost a week, Maureen told me." Phyllis's anxious gaze kept going to Alex. "I feel terrible I didn't come by with dinner sooner."

Jenny struggled to her feet.

"Now, don't go getting up on my account." Phyllis waved her to sit down. "I'll just leave this casserole and be on my way."

"You came all this way. Have a cup of coffee first." Jenny looked at Alex, assuming he'd reiterate the offer, but he said nothing.

Phyllis didn't seem to notice. "Well, I am a little parched."

Using her cane, Jenny limped toward her. "Come on. I usually make a pot around this time." She sniffed the air as she got closer. "That smells delicious. How sweet of you to think of us."

"It's nothing, really. Just a chicken and dressing casserole I whipped up. You've had it, Alex, at the Andersons' potluck last fall, remember?"

"Yeah, I remember."

At his less than enthusiastic tone, Jenny gave him the eye.

"Thanks," he added. "You really shouldn't have."

Jenny pressed her lips together to keep from laughing at the serious way he said that. Fortunately, again, Phyllis didn't seem to notice his disgruntled tone.

"Would you mind putting the dish on the counter?" Jenny asked as she slowly made her way to the kitchen.

"Of course I will." Phyllis hurried in front of her.

Jenny took the opportunity to whisper to Alex, "Quit scowling."

"Why did you ask her to stay?" he whispered.

"Shh! She'll hear you."

"Tough," he muttered.

Jenny giggled. This was so unlike Alex. It pleased her no end to see how truly annoyed he was that they'd been interrupted.

"This needs to be zapped in the microwave for only a few minutes whenever you're ready to eat," Phyllis said from the kitchen, oblivious to their private mutterings.

Jenny entered the kitchen and immediately went to the coffeepot.

"Oh, you shouldn't be walking around. Sit. I'll make the coffee." Phyllis didn't give her a chance to protest. The older woman snatched the basket of old coffee grounds, dumped them and put the basket under running water to rinse while she took off the plastic lid to the coffee can.

"Good for you, drinking a sensible brand of coffee," she said as she scooped grounds from the red can. "All those fancy new coffeehouse brands are a waste of money. Terribly overrated, if you ask me."

Jenny didn't argue. Not about making the coffee or being told to sit. She'd known Phyllis most of her life and knew better than to try to persuade her to change her mind about anything.

"I was shocked yesterday when Maureen mentioned you two were already back. Of course I'd been visiting my cousin just outside of Boston over the weekend, so I wasn't around."

Jenny craned her neck to look down the hall. Where the heck had Alex gone? He'd been right behind her.

"Do you remember her?" Phyllis continued as she filled the carafe with water. "My cousin Mabel lived here about twenty years ago. That was before she married that bum from Quincy. Thank God she left him five years ago. Took her long enough, if you ask me. Anyway, I was down there helping her plan her daughter's wedding when you got back, so that's why I hadn't heard—"

Phyllis stopped abruptly and turned to face Jenny. "For goodness sakes, I haven't even asked about the surgery. I'm so embarrassed."

"Don't be. I know Alex gave Maureen regular reports. I'm sure she kept you filled in." Jenny slid a furtive glance down the hall. She was more concerned about where Alex had gone.

"True. She said the surgery was a complete success and you could expect a full recovery."

Jenny nodded. "It's just a matter of time, going to physical therapy and doing my exercises. Which Alex makes sure I do even if I don't feel like it."

Phyllis frowned. "Where is that husband of yours?"

"I don't know. He was right behind me."

"Probably had to use the facilities." Phyllis went back to getting the coffee started. "Shall I stick this casserole in the microwave?"

"Not yet." Jenny bit her lip. She wasn't in the habit of telling fibs and she was horrible at it. But it would be for an excellent cause. "Alex said something about taking a nap before dinner. He had a long day at the clinic."

"Of course. He's probably so far behind on his work." Phyllis hurriedly washed and dried her hands. "I'll tell you what, honey. I'll stop by another time for a cup of coffee and a nice chat."

Jenny smiled with relief as Alex walked into the kitchen. He'd changed his shirt and combed his hair. His truck keys were in his hand.

"I wondered where you went," Jenny said lightly, while her heart sank.

"I got a call on my cell phone. I have to go back to the clinic." The way he averted his gaze indicated that her little white lie wasn't the only one told this evening.

"Oh, no. I'm sorry." Jenny gave him a sympathetic smile and then casually added, "Phyllis is leaving, too."

He looked briefly at Jenny, his expression unreadable. Did he understand that he didn't have to leave? That their evening hadn't been ruined? That within five minutes they could be naked and in bed together?

"Of course I could stay and keep you company awhile since Alex will be gone." Phyllis looked expectantly at her.

Jenny looked at Alex. They might as well have been discussing the weather for all the emotion he showed.

"Actually, I'm a little tired." Jenny gave the older woman an apologetic smile.

"Another time." Phyllis patted her arm. "Come on, Alex, I'll walk out with you."

"I'll call you later," he told Jenny, and stopped to give her a quick kiss on her forehead.

She tried to catch his eye, look for some sign that he'd hurry back as soon as Phyllis was gone. No luck.

"Thanks again for dinner," she called as Phyllis stepped outside. "I'll talk to you later, okay, Alex?"

"I'll call." He didn't turn.

Jenny went to the window and watched them both drive away. She got herself a cup of coffee and sat at the kitchen table, where she had a view of the driveway, and waited for Alex to return.

Two and half hours later, disappointed and confused, she gave up and crawled into bed.

CHAPTER TWELVE

THE NEXT MORNING Alex woke up early, before Jenny and the chickens, even though he hadn't gotten home and into bed until after midnight. Sleep hadn't come for another hour after that. And then it had been restless and fitful, and every time he had a conscious thought, it was about how much he wanted to have Jenny beside him in his bed.

He cursed to himself as he measured out the coffee grounds for the third go-round. He'd lost track at about the fifth scoop every time.

"You have some explaining to do, mister."

The sound of Jen's voice startled him, and half the grounds from the scoop ended up on the counter. "Damn it."

"That's the least of your worries."

He turned to find her standing in the doorway, her hands on her hips. "What's wrong?"

"What's wrong?" she repeated, her eyes wide with indignation. "You come home at some ungodly hour without calling, and you ask me what's wrong?"

She sounded so much like a wife that he smiled.

"You find worrying me amusing?" She wasn't just angry. Hurt resonated in her voice, dulled her eyes.

"You're right. I should have called." He narrowed his gaze. Something was different. "Your cane... you're not using your cane."

Her face brightened, and she smiled. "I can walk for short periods without it now."

"That's terrific, Jen." He put aside the coffee, ignoring the spill, and washed and dried his hands. "Just don't overdo it."

Her expression fell. "Yes, Dad."

He winced. "I worry about you."

"Tough. I worried about you last night." The hurt was in her eyes again.

He slowly walked toward her and watched the wariness creep into her face. He bracketed her waist with his hands. "I'm sorry, honey. That was childish."

She blinked. "Were you at the clinic?"

"Most of the time." He hesitated, not wanting to admit that he'd driven around like a lovesick teenager, pouting because they'd been interrupted yet afraid to finish what he'd started. But he didn't want to lie to her, either.

She let the silence stretch, waiting for him to explain. Her face was tilted to his, and her eyes were the most incredible caramel color. He slid his hands around her and drew her closer.

"Why did you stay away?" she asked with the earnestness of a child.

"Because I was a fool." He lowered his head, and she lifted her mouth for his kiss.

Her lips were soft and warm and incredibly sweet. They tempted him to forget that making love wasn't a good idea. She was too vulnerable. Hell, at this point, so was he.

He'd always liked and respected Jenny. She was smart and funny and ambitious. She hadn't forgotten her father just because she'd left the nest. She'd sent him money when she could, and her letters and phone calls were unfailing, no matter how demanding her career.

But who would've thought he could feel like this about her?

He didn't have a free moment when he didn't think about her. Even when he was tending patients, he sometimes had to focus his concentration. Jenny kept leaping into his thoughts.

He wondered what she was doing, whether she'd done her exercises. He worried that she was lonely or bored and missed New York. He dreaded the day she'd be well enough to leave.

The thought ignited a need in him so great, he abruptly deepened the kiss, mindless of her gasp of surprise. She didn't resist but ran her palms up his chest to encircle his neck. Her firm breasts pressed against him, and he fought the urge to pick her up and carry her to his bed.

She shifted suddenly, and he withdrew, anxious that he'd somehow hurt her. "Are you okay?" he asked, still holding her by the waist.

She nodded, her eyes dazed. "I think it's Bagel."

Alex shook his head. What the heck was she talking about? And then he heard the sound. Bagel was at the door, whimpering and scratching to come inside.

"Damn, I'd forgotten I let him out." He had no choice but to release Jenny. Bagel wouldn't give up until he was let in, and the scratching noise would drive them both crazy.

Jen reached for something on the other side of the door. It was her cane, which she'd left leaning against the wall. Alex gritted his teeth in annoyance. What a selfish jerk he was. She probably hadn't planned on standing unassisted that long.

"Better go let him in," she said. "Or you know he'll start barking loud enough to wake the entire county."

"Have a seat and I'll finish making the coffee." He opened the kitchen door and Bagel rushed in as if a fire burned on his heels. The dog headed directly for Jenny.

Alex was about to stop him, afraid he'd be too boisterous for her, but she put out her hand and rubbed the area above his nose and between his eyes, just where Bagel liked it.

"Well, good morning, boy. Did you have a good run? Huh?" She scratched behind one ear, then the other. Bagel curled into a ball at her feet. He was putty in her hands. Just like Alex.

JENNY WASN'T quite up to baking. Standing on her feet long enough to assemble the ingredients and then mix the dough would be foolish. Any other day she might have gone ahead and pushed herself. Not today, though. She had plans for tonight, and she wanted to be in tiptop shape.

After Phyllis Cooper's interruption last night and Bagel's intrusion this morning, Jenny didn't want anything getting in her way for the perfect dinner she had planned…and more important, for the rest of the night. They were going to end up in bed. Together. Her bed or his, it didn't matter.

But she had washed her sheets just in case. And sprayed the pillowcases with cologne. She'd dusted the various pictures and knickknacks she had scattered on her dresser and storage headboard. The chores had taken a lot of energy and effort. That was why she'd decided against spending too much time in the kitchen.

She picked up the phone and punched in the number for the local pizzeria. They had a few pasta dishes on the menu, and since they were the only establishment in the area that delivered, pasta would have to do. It was not being able to make a pineapple upside down cake that annoyed her. Alex had said it was his favorite. She'd really wanted to surprise him.

After she placed an order for lasagna and antipasto, she carefully studied the small assortment of wine Alex kept on an oak rack in the dining room. She selected a cabernet she'd seen him drink with pasta once before, then set the table with the good china.

At five-twenty, she ran a warm lavender-scented bath. He would be home at six-thirty, he'd assured her, which gave her enough time to bathe and put on some makeup and do her hair. She'd be so irresistible, nothing would stop him from taking her to bed.

Sometime around noon, after she'd gotten over hurt feelings from his disappearance last night, she'd come to a realization. She had to make the first move. The first real move. The take-no-prisoners move. Alex's misguided sense of honor was screwing everything up. He thought of himself as her protector. Her father's friend. Not as a potential lover. It would be up to her to prove he could have all those roles, if he chose.

She got out of her clothes and lowered herself into the warm sudsy water. This was her first bath since the surgery. She'd been afraid of slipping and hurting herself. Even now, the slick porcelain tub made her nervous, but she settled into the soothing water, rested her head against the air pillow and closed her eyes.

Although she'd brought a magazine to look at, she doubted she'd have time to read it. Her head was too full of hope and determination, a jumble of fear and doubt. Tonight she'd suggest more changes than sleeping in the same bed. She needed to have more to do during the day. And working at the clinic was a good solution.

Heather, Alex's part-time help, was going to be away for two weeks, touring potential colleges. Why should the clinic be shorthanded when Jenny was perfectly capable of pitching in? Alex would balk. If anything about him annoyed her, it was that he tried to coddle her too much. But she wouldn't take no for an answer.

The lavender-scented water did its job, the soothing bouquet calming her, giving her strength to confront Alex. No, not confront but persuade. He just needed a little push. The way he looked at her and kissed her and held her convinced her he felt the same way she did—at least about the physical side of their developing relationship. That belief gave her courage.

She tried to reach for the loofah sponge, but it was too far away. She lifted her foot out of the water to use her toes to snatch the sponge, and when that attempt failed, she stretched farther.

The action brought her scar in sharp contact with the tub and she winced. "Damn it!"

"Jen?"

Alex's voice made her straighten. What the heck was he doing here so early? She'd left the bathroom door open since she was home alone.

"Jen, where are you?"

"In the bathroom."

"Are you okay?"

"Fine."

"I heard you—" He stopped at the bathroom door and stared at the suds barely covering her breasts. "I'm sorry. I didn't know—" He started to back away.

"Alex, for goodness sakes, you're my husband, you can come in."

His startled gaze darted to her face. He said nothing, but of course she knew what he was thinking. Husband in name only. But something had changed between them in the past couple of weeks, and it was time to acknowledge the shift.

He stuck his hands in his jeans' pockets. "I had to drop off some medication for Ida Mann's cocker spaniel, so I figured I'd do it at the end of the day and come home early. I probably should have called first."

"Why?"

He shrugged and ran a restless hand through his hair. "So I wouldn't catch you by surprise."

"Unfortunately, my life isn't that exciting."

He gave her an odd, disgruntled sort of look. Did he think she was complaining?

"You're actually just in time," she continued casually, even though her insides did a nervous tap dance. "I was just wondering how I'd reach my back. Would you mind?"

"You mean—" He seemed reluctant, then he cleared his throat and glanced around the bathroom. "What did you want me to use?"

"I have this loofah sponge...." She tried to lean forward but thought better of it when the movement pulled at her lower back. "I dropped it in the water. I think it's somewhere by my feet, but it's hard for me to reach."

His eyebrows rose. "You want me to fish it out?"

She nodded. "If you don't mind."

Pushing back his sleeves, he crouched near the foot of the tub. He plunged his hand into the water and found her ankle. "Sorry," he muttered.

At the apprehension on his face, she hid a smile.

The next time he found her calf, then his hand traveled to her knee. She held her breath when he didn't immediately withdraw.

"I know it's down there somewhere," she said, her voice hopelessly shaky.

Alex's eyes met hers. "You're sure? Maybe I should stop searching."

"No, it's there." The suds had started to disappear around her breasts, and she didn't know if she should sink down into the water or sit up straighter.

She reclined a little more, and one of her nipples surfaced. Just barely, but enough to draw Alex's attention. He froze, his hand still submerged.

"Can't you find it?" she asked, her breathlessness giving her away.

"Jen, are you sure?"

"If it's in here?" She wasn't sure about anything anymore, least of all what they were talking about. She swallowed. "A little higher, Alex."

His hand left her knee, and she thought he was going to draw back, but he slid his palm up her thigh, his fingers trailing to the wet curls at the juncture.

She closed her eyes and held her breath.

"Am I getting warmer?" His voice was a low, hoarse whisper, and her breath shuddered in her chest.

"I am." Oh, God, had she said that out loud? She opened her eyes.

He smiled, his eyes ablaze with uncensored desire. His gaze stayed on her face as he slid a finger between her thighs. She tensed, and he slowed his hand. But as soon as she relaxed, he slid inside her, smooth and deep.

A whimper breached her lips and she bit the back of her hand to keep from crying out.

"Sweetheart?" His tone deep with concern, he started to retreat.

She lifted her hips, and his finger went in deeper. "Don't stop," she whispered. "Please."

A low guttural noise came from his throat, and he swooped down to capture her lips in a long, demanding kiss. Water splashed the front of his shirt when he traveled lower to take a nipple into his mouth.

"Alex, take off your clothes." She drove her fingers through his hair, bucking when he inserted a second finger and went deeper still.

"Relax, sweetheart." He kissed a path up her throat, along her jaw. "Just lie back and relax."

"I want you in here with me."

"The tub's too small."

"But I could—"

He shook his head and ran his tongue over her lips. "It's hard for me to get in by myself. I'll end up hurting you."

"I want to feel you against me. Your skin against mine. Your—" He withdrew his fingers, then slid them in with skilled purpose. "Oh." She couldn't remember what she wanted to say.

"In a minute, we're going to dry you off...." He kissed her behind the ear.

She let her head fall to the side.

"And then I'm going to pick you up...." He let

his tongue lightly trail across her jaw. "And carry you to bed."

She moaned.

"My bed," he whispered, and teased her lips open.

Her eyes drifted closed. She wanted to see the hunger burning in his eyes but she didn't have the strength to open hers. He hadn't stopped stroking her, and with the pressure continuing to build, she seriously thought she might be going out of her mind.

"You okay, sweetheart?" His voice was low and caressed her face, his warm breath offsetting the cooled water.

She realized she was moaning. She couldn't stop. Not when he touched her this way.

"Jen, let go." He kissed her briefly. "Come on, baby, let go."

She didn't want to climax alone. She wanted it to be with Alex. Naked. Beside her.

She bucked when a particularly strong wave overcame her. "Oh, oh…"

"That's right, baby. Come on."

There was a noise somewhere in the house. Or maybe outside. A ringing sound echoed in her head.

Another wave of sensation washed over her. And then another. She was drowning in it without a lifeline. No, Alex was there. Kissing her. Stroking her.

She clutched at his shirt as she exploded again.

The noise was louder now.

Bagel barked.

Alex muttered a curse. Strong words she had never heard him use before.

"I better get it." He withdrew his hand, then kissed her half on the mouth, half on the cheek. "It doesn't sound like they got the hint."

She blinked. The fog was still thick. "Who?"

"Someone's ringing the doorbell." He rose to his feet. The front of his shirt was soaked.

"It's the lasagna."

He pushed back the heavy wet strands of hair that hung in his face and narrowed his gaze.

She realized how weird that sounded. "I ordered takeout for dinner."

"Lasagna." He issued a humorless laugh. "Okay."

He left the bathroom, and she sank until the water met her chin. Damn doorbell. She couldn't even enjoy the afterglow of what Alex had—

The past few minutes finally and truly sank in, and she closed her eyes. He'd barely touched her, and she'd almost come apart. And he'd seen it. All of it…her every reaction. Every expression.

Oh, God.

She took several deep breaths, splashed cool water on her heated face. She shifted and could swear his fingers were still inside her. Closing her eyes, she cupped one breast and then the other, remembering the feel of Alex's hands on her body.

She thought she heard a noise, and her eyes flew open and she lowered her hands.

He stood over her, unbuttoning his shirt, his gaze on her breasts. "I put the lasagna and whatever else you ordered in the oven."

She could feel the pressure building between her thighs again, and he hadn't even touched her.

"Fine." She swallowed. "Are you coming in?"

He shrugged off his shirt, then extended a hand. "You're coming out."

A shiver skittered down her spine as she let him pull her to her feet. The cool air hitting her wet skin accounted for part of her reaction, but mostly it was the look on Alex's face as he ran his gaze down her body that had her trembling.

Once he got her out of the tub and steady, he grabbed a large plush burgundy towel off the rack and wrapped it around her as she faced him. He drew the terry cloth down her back, over her bottom and down her legs. On his way up, he kissed each of her nipples, and then her mouth.

She pressed against him, her breasts flattening on his solid chest as he kept his arms wrapped around her, slowly rubbing the towel over her heated skin. His belt buckle shoved into her flesh, and she reached between them to remove it.

With amazing efficiency she disengaged the buckle, but had trouble getting the zipper all the way down. He was too hard and thick, making his jeans snug. His kiss grew to a fevered pitch as she slipped her fingers inside his waistband and brushed the tip of his arousal.

"Jen." His warm breath branded her skin as he sucked and nibbled her earlobe. "Let's go to my room."

She could hardly breathe, much less answer. She

wedged her hand deeper into his jeans and stroked his length. He shuddered against her, his chest heaving, his breathing uneven.

Drawing back, he ran the towel over her belly, down her thighs, then cast it aside. When he made a move to pick her up, she stopped him.

"It's better if I walk." She kissed him briefly when he seemed hesitant, then took his hand.

He slid an arm around her waist and pulled her close to kiss the sensitive spot behind her ear. "Are you sure you don't want to save your energy?"

She smiled. He didn't fool her. The arm around her waist was a subtle attempt to lend support. Was there a more considerate man on earth? "I'll have plenty of energy for that."

He kissed her, then slowly led her out the door. They'd made it only halfway down the hall when a shrill alarm split the sensual silence.

CHAPTER THIRTEEN

ALEX JERKED AROUND. "What the hell is that? It sounds like a smoke detector."

"I don't know. Go see. I'll get a robe."

He headed down the hall while Jen slipped into her room. He could see the smoke even before he got to the kitchen. A little filtered into the hall, but as soon as he turned the corner he saw the thick, smoky fog shrouding the oven and microwave.

Ignoring the shrill alarm, he went straight for the oven, where it appeared the smoke came from, and opened the door. The foil and white cardboard box he'd placed inside smoldered, the corners charred and black.

He quickly turned off the oven and searched the drawers for a pot holder. He'd transferred the containers to the sink when Jenny appeared, wrapped in a fuzzy pink robe.

"What happened?"

He barely heard her above the shrill alarm. Another few inches and he could reach the smoke detector. Grabbing a kitchen chair, he climbed up and tried to disconnect the unit. With one good twist, the detector ended up in his hand—still buzzing.

"Damn it." He stared at it, wondering how to shut it off.

"Put it in here." Jenny opened the freezer door.

That startled a laugh out of him.

She took the detector out of his hands, put it in the freezer and shut the door. He could still hear the alarm, but it was pretty faint.

"Been there, done that. This is the only thing that works. Trust me." She pulled her belt tighter, her gaze going to the charred remains in the sink. "What happened?"

"I'm not sure. I put the lasagna and other stuff in the oven and..." He shrugged. "I don't know."

"Well, you must have turned the oven on too high."

"I don't remember doing that. Anyway, I'm sure I would have checked."

"The temperature was obviously too high."

His temper sparked. "Even if it was, it's not like I did it on purpose."

"I know." She made a sad face. "I'm sorry if I sound like I'm blaming you. It's just so darn—" She let out a low, frustrated shriek.

"Yeah, I know." He shook his head and opened the back door to get rid of the smoke. The situation would be comical if it weren't so damn irritating. Every time they started to get close, something happened. "Think somebody's trying to tell us something?"

"Definitely. To get away for the weekend." She turned on the stove vents while he opened a couple of windows. "Someplace where there are no talking birds or barking dogs or well-intentioned neighbors."

"You forgot smoke detectors."

"Unless we go camping, which I have no desire to do, we can't get away from them."

"But we can make sure a freezer is handy."

Her lips curved into a grudging smile. "Right."

He put his hands on her waist, and she moved closer. The top of her robe had fallen open, and he kissed the smooth silky skin above her breasts. Her soft sigh sent a bolt of need through him that nearly knocked him off his feet. He parted the robe further and touched the tip of his tongue to her nipple, so firm and ripe and tempting.

If she were in better health, he'd lay her across the table and take her right now. The desperation with which he wanted her scared the hell out of him. Drove away his good sense. But Jenny was an adult. She wanted him, too. Her feelings weren't simply about gratitude, as he'd originally thought—not the way she physically responded to him, the way she'd come apart with barely a touch.

Damn, but he wanted to bury himself inside her right now. Show her his need for her. But that wasn't going to happen. He kissed his way up to her throat, her jaw, her lips, then he pulled back.

She gave him a dazed look. "What's wrong?"

"Everything."

She blinked, and hurt filled her eyes.

"The smoke detectors are connected to the alarm

system, which I never use, except in the event of fire.''

"Meaning?"

"We're hooked directly to the fire station. They heard the alarm, too.''

"Can't you call them? Tell them it's not for real.''

He shook his head, wanting very much to punch a wall. "The system ties up the phone line for two minutes. They're already on their way.''

A second later they heard the sirens. He gathered the lapels of Jen's robe together to cover her. She half laughed, half groaned as she replaced his hands with hers and clutched the fabric.

"Why don't you go wait in your room while I take care of this?'' He kissed the tip of her nose.

"This weekend, you and me, we're outta here.''

He smiled. "Sure,'' he said, but he knew something else would come up. Fate obviously had other plans for them.

Maybe he should be grateful.

FOUR HOURS LATER, shortly after Alex had returned from a call to Floyd Webber's farm, Jenny made her way down the hall with only the soft yellow glow of the night-light to guide her.

"Alex?'' she whispered into the dark. He generally left his bedroom door open. She'd finally figured out that he did it because he wanted to be able to hear her if she needed him.

That was Alex, always kind and thoughtful. And damn, but he had magic hands.

"Alex, are you awake?"

"I'm awake." A dim light came on.

"Can I come in?"

He hesitated. "Sure."

She didn't like that he'd paused. In fact, it bothered her that he hadn't come to her room after returning home. Today they'd had a breakthrough in their relationship. She wasn't about to let him ignore it.

She stepped into his room. He sat up in bed, no shirt, the sheets pooled at his waist. She sucked in a breath. He had the best chest she'd ever seen. Or felt. Her palms itched to touch him again. And she would. Tonight. No question about it. For good measure, she'd already taken the phone off the hook.

"I'm sorry if I woke you when I got home," he said, his voice not sounding the least bit sleepy.

"I wasn't asleep." She moved into the room, wearing only a short nightshirt, and his gaze went to her bare thighs. "In fact, I was hoping you would come to see me."

"I thought about it."

"And?"

"I decided to leave you alone."

"Why?"

"Because you had enough—" He snorted. "Let's just say you had a rather full day and you need to rest."

"Do me a favor."

His brows rose.

"Don't decide what's best for me. I do that quite nicely." She got to the edge of his bed and trailed a finger down the valley in his chest to his waist. She heard his sharp intake of breath and slid her finger down another inch until it dipped beneath the elastic of his pajama bottoms.

"I wouldn't do that," he whispered hoarsely.

"Why not?" She slid a hip onto the edge of the bed. "Earlier you were ready to bring me here."

He moved over to give her room. "I had time to think."

"Bad idea. No thinking allowed."

One side of his mouth lifted. So did the sheet. If he tried to tell her he wasn't interested, she was fully prepared to be indelicate. "I want to make love to you, Jen. I won't deny it. That doesn't make it the right thing to do."

"You were ready to make love with me earlier."

"Like I said, I've done some thinking."

She crawled in beside him, resting her forearm and cheek on his chest. "And like I said, no thinking." She looked up at him. "For tonight, can we just feel?"

"Damn it, Jen, you make it so hard."

"My intention exactly."

When he got her meaning, he laughed and shook his head. He moved toward the center of the bed and pulled the sheet back in invitation.

She scooted closer to him, and he let the sheet fall over them.

He made sure she had a pillow. "Comfortable?"

"Very."

His large hand cupped her bare thigh. "You sure?"

"Positive."

"Even with all these clothes on?"

She smiled and reached for the hem of her night-shirt. He got to it first and slowly drew the shirt up her body and over her head. She really wished he'd just rip it off her, but she knew he wouldn't for fear of hurting her.

He threw the nightshirt on a chair then ran a hand down her side, over the curve of her hip. She snuggled closer, and he touched his tongue to her breast. He tried to slide his hand between her thighs, but she clamped them together. He tensed and started to withdraw.

"Not so fast, big guy." She hooked two fingers into the elastic waistband of his pajamas and tugged them down. "It's your turn."

He helped her by lifting his hips off the bed and kicking off the bottoms. Already fully aroused, he closed his eyes when she reached for him and ran her palm down his hard length. She encircled him with her hand, and he shuddered against her.

"Jen, let's go slow, honey." His words rasped against her skin as he kissed her shoulder.

"Slow?" She laughed softly. "We've been trying to get to this point for days."

He didn't laugh, but groaned as she stroked him. The powerful feeling his reaction gave her pumped her with courage. This was still new territory for her. Her limited sexual experience hadn't provided much reassurance. But with Alex, everything seemed right.

With him, she felt safe to experiment. If she blundered, they would only laugh.

She hoped.

Alex groaned and pushed into her palm. He slid a hand around her nape and pulled her to him for a deep, soulful kiss, then he released her and turned away. The loss she felt was so swift and devastating that it took her breath away.

He rolled over, reached into his nightstand drawer and brought out several packets of condoms.

"Oh." The heat returned, heading straight for the juncture of her thighs. "Alex, would you turn off the light?"

He touched the tip of her hardened nipple with the pad of his thumb. "Why?"

"Because."

"I love looking at you." He palmed her breast then dipped his head to lick the nipple. "You're so beautiful, Jen."

She wished he hadn't said that. Her old shyness and misgivings returned. "I don't want you to see the scar," she whispered, and snuggled into the pillow, hoping to hide the flush she felt climbing up her cheeks.

He tilted her chin and kissed her briefly. "Honey, the scar doesn't bother me. It's a part of you. It's a sign you're healing."

"Yeah, but it's pretty awful."

"I've seen it, Jen. It's not awful." He kissed her again, and she closed her eyes and focused on the feel of his mouth exploring hers and the way he rubbed his chest against her nipples.

"Please." She sighed when he finally broke the kiss and his lips teased the delicate skin of her throat. "Just this once, let's turn off the light."

He said nothing, but rolled over and extinguished the dim glow. She used the opportunity to find his arousal again, a little disappointed that she couldn't look at him.

"Jen…" Alex kissed behind her ear and down her neck at a fevered pace. "I'm not going to last if you keep doing that."

"Good."

Outside, Bagel barked. Too bad. She'd left him there so he wouldn't interrupt.

"Honey, wait." Alex tried to still her hand.

She'd have none of it. And then she heard the foil packet ripping. When he touched her hand, she let it fall away while he sheathed himself.

"I think it would be better if you're on top." He slid his hand over the curve of her hip.

She nodded, even though he couldn't see her, and slowly straddled him. He let her set her own pace, and when she finally sank onto him, she bit her lip to keep from crying out. Not in pain. But he felt so damn good inside her.

So right.

He moaned her name and cupped her breasts. She picked up the pace, and he filled her with such bliss she knew she was home. Where she wanted to be. Forever.

A NOISE woke Jenny. She blinked at the red glow of Alex's digital alarm clock. Two-thirty. How the heck could she have fallen asleep?

Beside her, Alex's chest rose and fell with his deep breathing. He still had one arm around her, and one of her legs was draped over his and her left hand rested on his firm stomach. She wanted to stay like this forever.

She swallowed a sigh, afraid of waking him. Of course Alex awake would be good, too. Heat surged through her at the memory of sitting on top of him, his arousal hot and heavy inside her.

She closed her eyes, savoring the memory.

Bagel barked.

Oh, God, the poor thing was still outside.

Jenny slowly pushed herself up and started to inch away from Alex.

"Stay here." His voice was thick with sleep, but his arm tightened around her.

"I'll be right back."

"Where are you going?"

Bagel barked again.

"Ah." Alex kissed her forehead. "I'll take care of him."

"No, I'm the one who left him out, and you have to work tomorrow." She tried to beat him out of bed, but he was quicker.

"Stay here. I'll be right back."

Her eyes had grown accustomed to the semidarkness, and she watched him go to his dresser and pull out a pair of boxer shorts. He really had a great body, so lean and firm, and she started to get hot and bothered all over again.

He stopped at the door. "Can I get you anything? Some water?"

"No, thanks. Just hurry back."

She thought she saw him smile. It was easy to imagine that sexy grin of his. And as much as she'd love to lie back and replay their earlier lovemaking in her head, a trip to the bathroom took precedence.

Foolishly forgetting about her back, she rolled over to the edge of the bed. Her foot hit the floor, and the unexpected pain made her wince. Caught off guard, she lost her footing and slid down the side of the mattress to the floor. A shooting pain brought tears to her eyes.

Clutching the quilt, she tried to struggle to her feet. Desperation and panic undermined her attempt, and she sat helpless and shaking. How stupid could she be? She should have been more careful. Tonight she'd used muscles that had been dormant since the surgery. Of course they'd give out.

Tears of frustration spilled down her cheeks as she tried to lift herself without success. She couldn't let Alex see her like this. He would blame himself. He would stay away from her, treat her as if she were too fragile to...

"Jen?" He flipped on the ceiling light.

She blinked at the brightness and covered her eyes with her hands. Her cheeks were wet beneath her palms.

In an instant, he crouched beside her and gently

tugged her hands away from her face. "What happened?"

"Nothing. I—I slipped."

"Oh, Christ."

"I'm okay. If you'd just help me up..."

"I'm going to call the paramedics."

She gasped. "Don't you dare! That's crazy."

"You don't understand, Jen. That's a big incision. You could have—"

"Either you help me up or I do it myself."

He hesitated. "I'm going to want to have a look at it."

"Fine."

"It might be easier if I pick you up."

"No. I'd rather you pull me to my feet."

He stood and took her hands. "Ready?"

She nodded and braced herself.

He slowly, gently pulled her up until she could stand on her own.

A pain shot up her spine, but she tried to keep a straight face. She even managed a smile.

"Okay?" he asked, his face so dark with concern it unnerved her.

"Yeah, but I have to go to the bathroom."

He nodded and took her elbow.

"I'm fine to go by myself."

"Now isn't the time to get stubborn, Jen." He looked different somehow. He wasn't her lover anymore, but her caregiver. She hated the transformation.

"Walk with me if you want. But I do have to go

now.'' Better to tell the small fib than to have him examine her.

He stayed beside her as she slowly made her way to the bathroom.

Once she got inside and closed the door, she looked over her shoulder into the mirror. The scar area was red, but it didn't seem worse. She'd bumped it good and would have been surprised if there had been no pain, but she'd really gotten to know her body, and she felt certain no damage had been done.

Satisfied and truly not too sore, she went about her business. When she was finished and opened the door, Alex waited just outside. Their eyes met, and she could see the regret in his. It went all the way down to his soul. The old cautious, reserved Alex was back. Couldn't they ever catch a break?

JENNY WAITED on hold for the fifth time. She didn't care. She was on a mission. So it was a busy weekend in Boston. There had to be one hotel room available. And she'd find it if it was the last thing she did.

As she waited, her gaze ran down the list of inns in the yellow pages. She'd briefly thought about booking a bed-and-breakfast an hour or so away from Cooper's Corner, but then decided that wouldn't do. Someone would find them. Or someone would know someone who knew Alex. They needed the anonymity of Boston.

They needed to stay in a place where Alex couldn't fabricate a distraction.

It had been two days since they'd made love. Two

days since she'd shared Alex's bed. He was back to being tentative around her, treating her with kid gloves, staying away for long hours but constantly calling to check on her. They barely had a moment's peace together.

An epidemic had obviously consumed the Berkshires. Every dog, cat and cow had some kind of ailment, and everyone called Alex. Tuck was gone for a few months. He had taken his family back to his ranch in Montana. He delayed his trip to help out at the clinic while Alex was in New York. But Alex had encouraged him to resume his plans and now Alex was working solo.

Nevertheless, she was relatively certain Alex encouraged the calls. He seemed to grab every distraction he could, anything that would keep him away from home.

The situation drove Jenny bananas.

She tapped the eraser end of the pencil on the kitchen table while she waited for the clerk to come to the phone. If this hotel didn't work out, she'd found a small inn to try right outside of Boston. Not her preference, but at this point, if a room was available, she'd take it.

The clerk came back, and again no luck. Jenny punched in the number to the inn. The woman who answered owned the place, and she had one room left to rent. Jenny grabbed it and was in the middle of giving her name and credit card information when Alex got home.

He smiled at her, laid his keys on the counter as

he always did, then went to the refrigerator for some water. That was his routine. He wasn't purposely listening to her conversation, she knew, but his curiosity had obviously been stirred.

He sat at the table as soon as she hung up.

"Hi, how was your day?" She gave him a bright smile as she gathered the phone book and her list of numbers with the directions to the inn she'd booked.

"Fine." His gaze went to her credit card and the paper on which she'd scribbled their confirmation number. "How was yours?"

"Busy."

"I see." He looked expectantly at her.

"I finally got reservations for the weekend," she said breezily.

"What reservations?"

"You know how we talked about getting away…"

His expression darkened. "That was before."

She widened her eyes, all innocence. "Before what?"

"Before you hurt yourself."

"Big deal. I slipped. Accidents happen. That didn't change anything."

He shook his head. "It's not a good idea."

"You can't keep me in a cage like Plato. I'm not going to break, and I can make my own decisions." She took a breath. "I *am* going away this weekend, and I really, really would like it if you came with me."

"But you'd go without me?"

She swallowed and nodded.

CHAPTER FOURTEEN

ALEX SET an extra pillow in the passenger seat of the car he'd rented for the weekend. Jen had insisted they take the truck. He'd proven he could be just as stubborn as she was. No way would he let her ride for three hours in that old truck with the worn shock absorbers.

As soon as they got back, he planned on looking for a new car. Maybe he'd trade the truck in on an SUV. The ride would be more comfortable for Jenny, yet he could still lug around all the stuff he needed for house calls.

But then again, in a few months, Jenny would be gone. Back to her old life, her old friends.

Which was for the best.

The night they'd made love had been a wakeup call. So damn bittersweet. One moment he'd thought he could never live without her and the next he knew, without reservation, that he could never open his heart to someone so fragile, a woman capable of wounding him deeper than the loss of Sara had already damaged him.

"You brought out another one?" Jenny stared at the pillows he was arranging. "There won't be any room for me."

"Good, we'll stay home."

She gave him a dry look. "You're welcome to stay home," she said sweetly. "I'll take my car."

"Yeah, right." They both knew her car was on its last leg.

"Oh, come on, Alex, we're going to have a great time." She tossed her small carry-on into the backseat.

"You should have let me bring that out for you."

"It wasn't heavy or I would have let you carry it." She gave him a serene smile, but her tone was anything but patient.

"Are you sure you want to do this?"

She glared at him. "If you don't get in the damn car right now, I will have to hurt you."

Alex couldn't help but smile. He still wasn't crazy about the idea, but he knew there was no way of stopping her once she had her mind set on something. At least he'd be there with her if she fell again or if anything else went wrong.

He waited until she got into the passenger seat and then closed her door. His bag was already in the trunk, and a small cooler with water and a couple of green apples was stowed on the floor behind his seat. He climbed in behind the wheel and had to clamp his mouth shut before he asked her again to reconsider this trip.

He had to get over his anxiety. He wasn't fooled. Her fall and the way she'd started limping had triggered some old feelings that had to do with Sara and when she'd gone from her short remission to chemotherapy. Jenny wasn't sick like Sara had been. This was a totally different situation. But he wished Jenny would take her recovery more seriously. If anything happened to her...

He put the mental brakes on. He couldn't think about that possibility. Couldn't afford to. Anyway, she wasn't his responsibility. So why did he feel so torn up inside?

Jenny didn't say a word for the first twenty minutes of the drive. She studied Alex's profile as he drove, painfully aware of the way he gripped the wheel, of the tension radiating from him. She felt so damn helpless. This was about her, of course. He was worried, and she figured a lot if that had to do with the torment he'd gone through with Sara.

At one point, two miles from the house, she'd almost given in and told him to turn back. But she knew that wasn't the answer. In fact, the surrender could make things worse. The night they'd made love, she'd decided she wanted to make their marriage real.

She believed that he did, too. But he was scared, and she didn't blame him. He'd suffered a devastating loss. Just because they were sexually compatible didn't mean anything. Part of him probably didn't want to make their arrangement permanent. He still worried about her being sick. It didn't matter that she was healing, that her recovery would be complete. She was breakable in his mind, and that equaled loss.

Until she convinced him she wasn't going to shatter and break if he touched her, until he looked at her as a woman, not a sick woman, they didn't have a snowball's chance in hell of succeeding.

Damn, but she wanted this to be a real getaway, a chance to mend for both of them. The way Alex continued to stare straight ahead, his jaw set, it looked as if it were up to her to break the ice.

She thought for a moment and then asked, "How's Zeus doing?"

He gave her a startled look before returning his gaze to the road. "Fine."

She rolled her gaze skyward. "Could you be a little more brief?"

Alex slanted her another look, this one amused, at least. "He's getting around more, but he's still learning to compensate for the loss of his paw."

Better. At least it wasn't a one-syllable answer. But she didn't want to have to drag every word out of him. They sat in bucket seats, but she scooted as close to him as she could and laid a hand on his thigh.

He jerked and gave her a sharp look.

She took a deep breath. In for a penny... "Okay. Question. What's the wildest place you've ever made love?"

The car swerved to the right. "What?"

"Don't be a spoilsport."

"What kind of crazy question is that?"

"Come on, there's no place to run, and I won't let you hide. Out with it."

He shook his head. "You're insane."

"Yep. Certifiable." She squeezed his thigh. "But

I'm also stubborn. I suppose I should warn you. I have ways of making you talk.''

He laughed. ''All right already. I'm thinking.''

Jenny settled back and smiled. Amazing how talk of sex was a surefire icebreaker. Talk of sex, hints of sex. Anything that had to do with sex automatically started the ball rolling.

''Okay.'' His mouth curved into a playful grin. ''I once had sex in a bathtub.''

Disappointed, Jenny snorted. ''A bathtub?'' Was he referring to the two of them a few nights ago? ''That's not so wild.''

''Yeah?'' He slid her a brief look before changing lanes. ''The bathtub was in a model home during an open house.''

She gasped. ''Alex McAlester, you didn't.''

He shrugged. ''You asked.''

''Okay, you're right. That is wild.'' She laughed. The admission was so unexpected.

''Your turn.''

''That wasn't the deal.''

''Jen…'' He drawled her name in warning.

''Okay, but I've got to think about this.''

He grunted.

''I'm not kidding.'' She shifted, suddenly uncomfortable with the game. ''I was a late bloomer, and anyway, I've really never gone for casual sex.''

''I didn't know we were talking about casual sex.''

''Okay, but it's not like I've had a lot of relationships.'' She folded her arms across her chest. ''I was busy working.''

"Right. You have five seconds."

She made a sound of exasperation. "You don't believe me."

"I didn't say that, but I'm sure you've had at least one unorthodox encounter."

"That's a fancy way of putting it."

"One second remaining."

She laughed. "All right. It was on the roof of my building one summer—right around sunset. It was getting dark, and I didn't think anyone could see us, but when we, um, well, when we'd finished, someone, somewhere applauded."

Alex laughed so hard he had to slow the car down.

"It wasn't funny. I was never so humiliated in my life."

He reached over and took her hand, and the tension between them seemed to evaporate. "It's funny now."

"Yeah, I guess." She held on to his hand, enjoying his touch. His skin was warm and his grasp reassuring. So much better to feel than to think. Thinking made her too aware of the obstacles in their way. "Okay, now you get to think of a question."

"Hmm, let me think."

"Don't get carried away."

"You ask me where I had the wildest sex and then tell me not to get carried away?" The mischievous glint in his eyes made her nervous. "What's your most wicked fantasy?"

Jenny's eyes widened. "You've got to be kidding."

"Nope."

"Come on, that's too intimate a question."

One side of his mouth lifted. "And your point is?"

She frowned. He was getting way too much into this game. Of course this was what she wanted, wasn't it? This sexy man-to-woman talk instead of the caregiver-to-sick-person mumbo jumbo. But tell him her wildest fantasy? Oh, God.

She could make something up.

"I'm waiting."

She cleared her throat. She hadn't even opened her mouth yet, and heat filled her cheeks. "No censure, right?"

"Nope. Tell it like it is."

"I meant from you."

"Oh." He laughed. "I won't say a word. Quit stalling."

She cleared her throat again. "I've always fantasized about—okay, now this isn't politically correct..."

"Jen, it's only fantasy. Just say it."

"I've thought about being swept away by a stranger. Someone tall and not too dark." Her little joke fell flat. "Being sort of, well, helpless."

His jaw tensed, and he shifted slightly in his seat. "Go on."

She didn't know how to read him. Did he think she was just awful? "That's all."

The look he gave her said everything. He didn't disapprove, he was turned on. "There's got to be more to the fantasy."

She hesitated, the heat still stinging her cheeks. "Are you shocked?"

He shook his head.

"Maybe a little?"

Alex smiled. He'd been mildly surprised but more excited than anything else. He wouldn't admit either to her. Nor that he was so hard and ready he'd like nothing more than to pull over and make love to her right now.

Of course he wouldn't, and not just because they were on the freeway.

Her hand moved on his thigh, and he sucked in a breath. She had to see he was hard. His jeans were so damn tight he thought he'd explode. How could he subtly tell her to stop? That she was making him crazy?

"Your turn," she said, finally stilling her hand. "Tell me your fantasy."

"You aren't done." Was he a masochist? Did he really want to hear more? Could he take any more?

"Oh, yes, I am." She laughed, her cheeks a becoming pink.

He grumbled under his breath, and she moved her hand up his thigh again. Man, he would probably regret this. "You're my fantasy." He kept his eyes off her and on the road. He couldn't believe he was making the admission. "I want to make love to you. All night long. I want to use my mouth. Taste every inch of you."

Jenny sighed. "You have to know you're my fantasy, too. You're sweeping me away right now. I've missed you these past two nights.''

He took one hand off the wheel and touched the silk of her hair, the satin of her cheek. ''I should be shot for expanding this conversation. We have another hour before we get to Boston, and if we don't change the subject, we're liable to end up in a ditch somewhere.''

As if to confirm his words, someone honked behind them when he swerved.

She laughed. ''Okay, hands on the wheel, eyes on the road.''

''Hey.'' He gave her hand a pointed look when she squeezed his thigh. ''Hands off me.''

''Whatever you say, Doc.'' She grinned and folded her hands in her lap. He was tempted to recant when she added, ''There is something else I wanted to discuss, and now that I have your undivided attention...''

Something in her tone made him uneasy. ''I'm listening.''

''I was thinking that I could be of help at the clinic.''

Was she serious? He darted her a look. Her earnest eyes met his before he returned his attention to the road. The idea was ridiculous. She needed to stay home, do her exercises and concentrate on getting well.

''What do you think?'' She sounded so tentative he didn't want to burst her bubble and come right out and say no. ''I know what you're thinking,'' she added, "but I am well enough. I wouldn't overdo it. Maybe I could start off working a couple of hours a day."

"I don't know, Jen. I really have to think about this."

"What's there to think about? You could use the help when Heather's away. And even when she's there, you've complained she can't keep up."

Hell, if he said no, there'd be a war. If he said yes, he'd be worried about her all the time. "Sometimes there's lifting involved. Heavy cages with dogs in them."

"And?" She had that stubborn frown on her face. Worst, she looked disappointed.

He sighed. "And either Tuck or I can do it."

"Really? Are you saying you agree?"

"No, I don't agree, but yes, you can work at the clinic if you want."

"Thank you, Alex." She kissed his cheek. "You won't regret this."

Right. He already did.

"IT'S A NICE ROOM, isn't it?" Jenny pushed aside the blue floral drapes. "Look, we can see the lake from here."

"Why don't you sit down while I unpack?"

"Because I've been sitting for three hours." She knew he meant well, and that was the only reason she hadn't wrung his neck. "I'll unpack my own things. I didn't bring much."

She took one last look at the lake then let the

drapes fall into place. They weren't really in Boston, but outside the city a few miles. And the lake wasn't really a lake, more like a man-made pool, but that was okay. She was just so darn happy to be here. Alone with Alex.

She picked up her carry-on and hoisted it onto the queen-size bed.

"I wish you'd let me do that," Alex grumbled.

"I'm sorry. I should have. But it wasn't heavy." She gave him a smile and slid her arms around his waist, tilting her head to look at him. "Don't be grumpy."

His gaze lingered on her mouth. "I'm not grumpy."

"Are you hungry?"

Amusement lit his eyes but only for a moment, then they darkened. She knew damn well what he was hungry for.

"I am," she said quickly, and stepped away from him before she gave in and they climbed into bed. Better to make him wait. Let him think about the weekend ahead and how much they can enjoy each other if he lets go. "I saw a cute little café about a block from here."

"Wouldn't you rather just have something in the room?"

She realized with disappointment that the desire in his eyes had been replaced by concern. He wanted to stay in because he thought she might be unwell. Not to do wicked things with her. She'd see about that.

''Nope. I'd like to eat out. Anyway, the walk will do me good.''

''Walk? Why can't we drive?''

''You can if you want.''

He wanted to argue. It was written all over his face. To his credit, he said nothing. He finished unpacking and waited for her to do the same without offering to help.

Good sign.

Their walk to the café was short, but the uneven sidewalk made the trek a little uncomfortable. Alex had to know it was difficult for her, but he said nothing, only offering his arm as any man would do.

Eating out was fun, and the double entendres throughout the meal were the best kind of foreplay. They laughed and ate and talked until all they were the only two lunch patrons left. The walk back went slower, but not until they got to the room did Alex ask how she was doing.

She kissed his cheek. He got A for effort.

''I'm a little sore, as expected,'' she admitted, ''but otherwise I feel terrific. But I do think I'll take a nice warm bath. That should fix me right up.'' She moistened her lips. ''But I'll probably need some help. You know, scrubbing my back or searching for sponges.''

The desire that flared in his eyes pleased her. He obviously remembered the last bath. So did she, and the memory made her body start to burn.

''You get your stuff, and I'll start running the water.''

''Thanks.'' She exhaled slowly. He hadn't been in

the bathroom yet so he hadn't seen the tub. She had, and she wondered if he'd have the same idea.

She went about the business of getting out the bath scents and candles she'd brought with her. It was the last of her stash from better days when she didn't have to eke out dollars from her meager savings. She heard the water running and wondered what the heck he was doing in there. Stalling, she got her new teddy and matching black lace panties, then wrapped them in a towel along with the candles so he wouldn't see them yet.

She was going to seduce him into that tub with her if it was the last thing she did. He'd balk, afraid he'd hurt her. But the size of the tub was to her advantage. Three people could fit in that monster.

When he still hadn't come out, she carried her things with her to the bathroom, knocking briefly at the open door.

"Alex, what are you—" She froze when she saw him reclining in the tub, wearing nothing more than a grin.

CHAPTER FIFTEEN

"YOU'RE STILL working here, huh?" Phyllis Cooper set her parakeet cage on the clinic's reception desk.

"Yup." Jenny smiled. "It's been two months now."

"And you haven't gotten divorced yet." Phyllis chuckled, and Jenny's heart thudded. "Good for you. Some people think husbands and wives shouldn't work together, that it's a shortcut to divorce court. Don't believe them. Philo and I have been running that store together for nearly thirty years." She narrowed her gaze and leaned closer to Jenny. "The trick is knowing when to give each other space."

Jenny smiled again. This was not a conversation she wanted to have. She knew about giving each other space. Sometimes Alex gave her too much of it. Maybe they needed another weekend getaway. Two months later, memories of Boston still had the power to make her knees weak.

Alex had been so sexy and demanding and giving. They'd barely left the room, and that had been okay with her. But as soon as they'd returned, something changed.

They still made love, and most nights she slept in

his bed. But the nights she didn't, the nights he came home inexplicably late and claimed he hadn't wanted to disturb her when he slept on the couch, she felt the distance between them.

"So what's wrong with Pierre?" Jenny asked, picking up a pen. She'd already pulled the bird's chart. Phyllis loved fussing over him, and he'd become a frequent patient.

"I think it's his ears. He may have a little infection or something."

Jenny peered closer. Did birds have ears? She'd find out soon enough. Amazing how much she'd learned from Alex in the past two months—more than she had growing up on a farm.

"I don't think he can hear me." Phyllis sighed. "He used to respond to my voice. Philo thinks Pierre's fine and he's just ignoring me. Like Philo does."

Jenny bit down on her lip to keep from laughing. Phyllis was totally serious. "Alex is in with a patient now," Jenny said, studying the appointment book. "But I'm pretty sure he'll have time to look at Pierre if you wait."

"Oh, bless you. That would be wonderful." Phyllis stayed at the counter. Jenny had hoped she'd take a seat in the waiting area. "How have you been feeling? You look good."

"I feel good. This is my last week of physical therapy."

"Oh, my, that was fast."

"I've healed so well and my range of motion has

improved enough that my doctor said I could do the exercises at home.''

''Good for you. I'm sure Alex is pleased.''

Jenny smiled dutifully. She wished she could be so certain. He hadn't responded to the news as she'd expected.

In fact, to her disappointment, he'd hardly reacted at all.

''He should be pleased,'' Jenny joked. ''Now that Heather is leaving, he'll need someone full time.''

Phyllis frowned. ''I thought Betty Mae's girl was going to take the job. She graduated from high school last spring.''

Jenny's chest tightened. Alex hadn't said anything. She'd assumed... Oh, God, she didn't feel well all of a sudden.

''Maybe I'm wrong.'' Phyllis pursed her lips. ''But I could've sworn Betty said Cindy would start here after she got back from her graduation trip to Boston.''

Jenny looked at her watch. ''Oh, gosh, I'm late.'' She laid down her pen, scrambling to think of an excuse. The hell with it. Phyllis didn't have to know where she was going. Especially since Jenny herself had no idea. ''Alex should be done in a minute,'' she said on her way to the door.

At Jenny's abrupt departure, Phyllis's brows rose. ''Okay. Nice talking to you.''

''Same here.'' Jenny forced a smile, stepped outside and took a deep breath of the crisp fall air. Not paying attention, she nearly tripped on the stone step to the walkway.

She hurried to her car, got in behind the wheel and stared at the thicket of maple trees behind the clinic. The whole wooded area had become a kaleidoscope of yellows and oranges. The scene was so beautiful it took her breath away. She often sat for a few minutes before or after work, just meditating. How could she not have appreciated growing up here?

She closed her eyes. How could Alex not have told her he was replacing Heather with someone else? The thought stung. She knew there were invisible barriers between them. She often felt him distancing himself, but she hadn't really gotten the impression he was anxious for her to leave when she was well enough.

Until now.

Why else hadn't he consulted her about Heather? He knew Jenny would stay to help out if he asked her. They got along well professionally. They'd had only one real disagreement—over Zeus's treatment. She respected Alex's medical knowledge, and as far as she was concerned, he was the best. But on a personal level, a human level, he held back. He let fear form his opinions.

Zeus should have been allowed to run on his own already, but Alex advised against it. He was too protective, the way he was with the people close to him. Sara's death had made him cautious, though he'd denied the possibility and become defensive when Jenny pointed it out.

But other than that one discussion, they never had

cross words or got on each other's nerves. Everything seemed to be going really well. Or so Jenny thought.

She felt in her pocket for her keys. Heather would be here within a half hour. Jenny didn't need to stick around. Apparently, Alex didn't need her at all.

She blinked away the threat of tears and started the car. A warm lilac-scented bath would make her feel better. So would Alex declaring his love for her. But that wasn't going to happen.

JENNY'S CAR was in the drive, but the kitchen was dark and so was the rest of the house. Alex flipped on the light switch, his stomach in knots.

"Jen? Where are you?"

No answer.

God, if anything had happened to her...

He flew down the hall and saw light flickering from the guest bathroom. "Jen?"

"Yes."

He briefly closed his eyes and sent up a prayer of thanks. "Are you all right?" he asked, hovering near the door.

"Of course." She sighed. "You can come in, Alex."

He stepped inside. She was lying in the tub, her head resting on her blow-up bath pillow, half a dozen candles glowing around her. Her hair was piled on her head, and her face was freshly scrubbed. She looked so damn beautiful.

"I tried calling."

"Sorry, it must have been while I was napping. I unplugged the phone."

That wasn't like her. He breathed deeply and moved into the bathroom. He put down the toilet lid and sat beside her. "You left the clinic so abruptly, I was worried."

"You don't need to worry about me, Alex." She flashed him a smile, a phony one. Her blasé tone, her indifferent expression, everything about her this evening put him on alert.

He brushed the back of his hand down her cheek, and her eyes drifted shut. "Of course I worry about you."

Her eyes flew open, and annoyance flickered in them. "How's Zeus? You were with him when I left."

Great. Not a subject they did well on. He withdrew his hand. "Okay. He's getting more confident and active." He knew what she was really getting at. She thought he was too protective, that Zeus should be allowed to roam Sylvia's property with the other dogs, as he had before. Alex knew better. Hadn't Sylvia gone through enough heartache with that dog? Why tempt fate?

Jenny didn't say anything. She played with the suds covering her breasts, giving him little peeks and shooting his blood pressure up.

"Jen, is anything wrong?"

"No, why?"

"You seem so...I don't know. Melancholy."

She sighed. "Maybe I am a little." She raised sad

eyes to him. God, he wished she'd tell him what was wrong. "Alex, take your clothes off."

He smiled. "Take my clothes off?"

She didn't smile, just nodded.

"Okay." He unbuttoned his shirt while she watched. And then he unzipped his jeans and kicked off his shoes. "You know I can't fit in that tub with you."

"I know." Her gaze stayed on him. She still seemed sad. He hoped it was the way the light from the candles flickered across her face that made her look that way.

He got rid of his socks and jeans and stood in his boxer shorts. Her eyes went to his face. He didn't move but held her gaze, waiting for further instruction.

"Finish undressing," she whispered, her gaze dueling with his, challenging him to a game he didn't understand.

He slid down the shorts and exposed his arousal. He was so hard and ready he worried he'd embarrass himself. The way she stared at him didn't help, her lips parted, her eyes glassy with desire.

"Come here." He held out a hand to her.

"Why?"

He raised his eyebrows. "Because I can't get in there with you."

A slight smile curved her mouth, and she lifted a hand to cup one of her breasts. "So?"

His entire body reacted to the sensual move. "Jen, you're being sadistic."

She laughed softly. "For better or for worse, remember?"

His heart thudded. Her tone, her words—they were more effective than a dousing of cold water.

She moved the hand from her breast and touched the tip of his arousal. He was still hard, in spite of what she'd just said, and if she kept stroking him the way she was doing, he'd stay that way. But she released him and took his hand.

When he realized she was starting to lift herself out of the tub, he pulled her the rest of the way up, drawing her flush against him. He kissed her hard and deep, and she responded with a desperation that aroused him even more.

He grabbed a towel and quickly dried her off, kissing her throat and breasts as he did. All he could think of was burying himself inside her, reassuring himself she was still here with him.

As soon as she was dry, he picked her up and carried her to his bedroom. When he laid her on the bed, she wouldn't let go of his neck, so he sprawled out beside her. He greedily suckled her breasts and slid a hand between her thighs.

"I want you inside me," she whispered. "Now."

He kissed her one more time on the mouth before grabbing a condom from the nightstand. The entire tone of their lovemaking was different, more desperate, urgent, and yet he wanted to take his time, taste her heat, make her climax over and over again.

She'd have none of it. She was too impatient. She spread her thighs and tried to guide him to her. He hesitated. She always straddled him so her back wouldn't feel any pressure.

"It's okay," she whispered. "I promise."

He started to protest.

She put a finger to his lips. "I want you on top of me. Inside me. Now."

He had to trust that she knew what she was doing. Slowly, he stretched out over her, careful not to let her absorb too much of his weight.

She didn't seem concerned but wrapped her legs around him, kissed him passionately while reaching between them to guide him inside her. Her impatience fueled his hunger, and he had to concentrate, force himself to go slow and not plunge hard and deep.

But Jenny cupped him from behind and drew him to her while she lifted her hips and ground against him. He couldn't think, couldn't articulate his concern. If she didn't stop, he'd explode at any moment.

Jenny reveled in Alex's weight on top of her, the thick heaviness inside her. How right he felt. How perfect they were together. She closed her eyes and pressed harder, wanting him buried as deep inside her as possible. She wanted to pretend he'd never let her go.

She opened her eyes to find him watching her, his dark gaze unwavering. Unreadable. And then he plunged inside her, and she clung to his shoulders and kissed his neck as the pressure built.

Alex groaned, and she knew he was close to climaxing. So was she. She lifted her lips for his kiss, and in the next instant a wave of sensation and emotion washed over her. Her muscles clutched him. He tensed, plunged into her again and cried out her name.

Jenny just wanted to cry. She loved Alex. With all her heart. And she had no idea what she was going to do about it.

"WHERE are you going?"

He hesitated at the edge of the bed. He thought she'd fallen asleep. "The candles are still burning. I'm going to put them out."

"Will you come right back?" Her voice was soft and unsure, not at all like the woman who'd driven him crazy for the past hour.

He leaned across the bed and kissed her parted lips. "I'll only be a minute."

She smiled and snuggled into the pillow.

Alex couldn't wait to get the hell out of the bedroom. As soon as he closed the door to the bathroom, he splashed cold water on his face, then stared at himself in the mirror.

What the hell did he think he was doing? Hadn't he told himself to keep things cool? To not get in too deep?

Too deep. What a joke. He was in so deep it would take a miracle to crawl back out. And it was wrong. So damn wrong. He liked Jenny and he wanted her well and happy. But he liked her too much. That was the problem. Because once she was well, she'd leave.

Cooper's Corner could never offer her enough opportunity and excitement. Neither could he. Jen had become a sophisticated city girl, and he was a country vet, and their whole arrangement was about health insurance and getting Jenny on her feet. How could he have stupidly lost sight of that reality?

He should have known better. It wasn't difficult to get swept up in the illusion. It was natural, of course, living with each other, pretending to be married—it all made the illusion seem so real.

But there was more—his own failing, his inability to let himself get close to anyone. When Sara had died, it tore him apart. He thought he'd healed. But having Jen in his life brought back bad memories, triggered negative responses he thought he'd put behind him.

It wasn't as if he couldn't enjoy her company or their time together. He thought about making love to her all day, even while he was at the clinic. It was pathetic, at his age, having this sexual obsession like some teenage boy.

But as long as he didn't get caught up in the fantasy, he'd be okay. They both would. Jenny wasn't looking for a white picket fence in Cooper's Corner. This was a port in the storm for her, and the storm was almost over.

He finally remembered he'd come in to douse the candles. All but one had already burned down. He put out the remaining flame and took a deep breath. He'd been gone too long. She had to be wondering what had kept him.

If he were truly an honorable man, he'd stay the hell away from her. It didn't matter that she was a willing participant or that she'd been rather forward in bringing their relationship to a sexual level. Alex was supposed to be the strong one. He should have put the brakes on.

But God help him, he couldn't stay away. Maybe for a day or two, but then he'd come crawling back to her. It was going to be a hell of a lot easier once she was gone and he could go back to his old life of quiet, predictable solitude. Much easier. So why did the thought make him feel so damn hollow inside?

JENNY HEARD him return, but she stayed on her side, deep under the covers, facing away from him. The mattress dipped with his weight, and when he touched her shoulder, she dabbed at her cheek in case a stray tear had fallen.

Something was wrong. She'd felt it before he went to the bathroom. It was that invisible wall he seemed to randomly erect. How could he have done that right after they'd made love?

His warm fingers lingered on her shoulder. "Are you awake?"

"No."

He laughed. "Okay, so that was a stupid question." He paused when she refused to turn around. "Tired?"

"A little," she said, and immediately felt his withdrawal.

"Why don't you take a nap?"

It was dinnertime. She should get up. Or ask him to join her. He wouldn't. He'd be afraid to touch her. Hell, she couldn't even be tired without him thinking she was sick.

"Yeah, I think I will."

"Jen?"

She held her breath. His tone was low, intimate, almost a caress. The way a man speaks when he tells a woman he loves her. "Yes?"

"Maybe you should cut back your hours at the clinic."

She turned her face deeper into the pillow and swallowed a sob. "We'll talk about it later."

"Sure." The mattress shifted as he rose. "Get some rest."

She said nothing and kept her face buried while she listened to him get dressed. She loved him. He didn't love her, and the truth hurt like hell.

It wasn't his fault. He'd stuck to the rules. She was the one who'd gotten foolishly emotional. But she wouldn't make things difficult for him. She'd be the same old Jen as always, and in the next couple of months, maybe sooner, she'd make arrangements to leave.

Steven had called and given her a line on a job. The position wasn't anything great, and the pay was mediocre, but he'd also offered her his apartment while he and Brian were in Europe for two months. A temporary solution, but at least it would allow her to leave Cooper's Corner, let Alex get back to his real life.

The thought of leaving hurt more than a physical blow, and she huddled deeper still, pulling the covers to her chin.

"Jen?" Alex touched her shoulder again, then

combed his fingers through her hair. "I'm going to run into town. Do you need anything?"

She shook her head. He probably expected her to turn around and kiss him or say something, but she couldn't. He'd know she'd been crying.

He let his hand trail down to her shoulders, and he gently rubbed her back a moment. "I'll be right back."

She swallowed hard. "Okay." Her voice was muffled under the sheet.

He hesitated, and then she sensed that he'd moved away from the bed. When he got back, she would be in her room. He wouldn't bother her. He'd let her be. And even if she stayed in his room, it wouldn't matter. The wall had effectively come up between them.

CHAPTER SIXTEEN

ALEX ALWAYS tried to see his last patient by noon on Saturdays. Today he finished at eleven-thirty, so he locked up the clinic, checked to make sure his pager was on and headed home.

Jen's car was in the drive. He'd hoped she'd be home from the market. She'd become unpredictable in the past month, going out at odd times, taking long drives by herself, almost as if she were testing him.

Or trying to keep her distance.

He couldn't fault her for that, but he didn't like it. Even though it made sense. Even though he did it himself. When the hell had life gotten so complicated?

He came in through the kitchen door and paused to throw his keys on the counter. Music blared from the living room—an oldies radio station they both liked.

Curious, he headed toward the music, then froze at the living room entryway. Jenny sang and danced to the Latin beat. The way she moved took him by surprise. She swayed her hips and moved her feet to the rhythm. How long had she been able to dance like that?

He knew she'd stopped her physical therapy a month ago, but since she was still doing her exercises at home, he hadn't taken the next logical step. She wasn't a hundred percent yet, but she was almost there. Well enough to work, of course. Well enough to make love.

Well enough to leave.

His heart fell to his stomach, and his chest tightened painfully. Had his denial been that strong that he couldn't see how much better she'd gotten? But it was too soon. The doctor said recovery would take longer…a few more months at least…

Jenny turned and saw him. She jumped, putting a hand to her throat. "You scared the heck out of me."

He stood there, speechless. He didn't know what to say.

She frowned and lowered the radio volume. "What's wrong?"

Alex shook his head. For the life of him he couldn't think of a thing to say. What was there to say, anyway? Don't go? Stay here in this Podunk town, keep working in my little clinic, be my wife forever, and by the way, never get sick again?

"Alex?" She walked to him, fear and concern in her eyes. "Please tell me what's wrong. You look— awful."

He shook his head again. "I'm fine."

"No, you're not."

Her face was filled with so much worry it made him angrier with himself. He was the strong one, the one who was supposed to worry. Not her. He had to pull himself together.

Jen took his hand. Hers was so warm it gave him comfort. "Come sit with me."

He let her lead him to the couch, and they sat. Close. Closer than they had in two weeks.

"Alex, you're frightening me. Please tell me what's wrong."

He shrugged, trying to look blasé. "I just didn't expect to see you dancing."

Jen blushed. "That wasn't dancing, exactly. I was just swaying and moving, sort of getting familiar with my body again." She squeezed his hand. "I've been so out of step with myself, pardon the pun." She smiled. He tried and failed. "It seems the only time I'm at peace with myself physically is when we make love."

Her cheeks got pink again, and she looked at their joined hands.

He lifted her chin. "I don't understand. But I want to."

"It's hard to explain."

"Will you try?"

"Getting sick like I did and then finding the tumor, well, it seemed like a betrayal. I know that probably doesn't make sense to you." She shrugged and looked away. "But I'd always been healthy and strong and in charge of my life. And then everything got turned upside down."

He squeezed her hand encouragingly. It was beginning to make sense.

"Getting sick seemed like a punishment, but I didn't know what I'd done wrong. And the punishment kept coming. I lost my job. I had no resources to get the medical attention I needed." Her lips curved in a faint smile. "And then you came along, and things started to get better, but I'd already lost touch with myself. The surgery, the recovery period—all were necessary, but they further distanced me from myself." She made a face. "This probably isn't making any sense to you."

He stared blankly at her. All he could think about was how she'd referred to her recovery period in the past tense. It was over. Really over. Jenny was well. She didn't need to stick around anymore.

"I told you it was hard to explain," she said, pulling her hand away and hugging herself. Her cheeks had gotten pink again, and she seemed embarrassed.

"I'm sorry. It does make sense, and I was just processing what you said." God, he was such an ass. What a traumatic time she'd had, and all he could think about was himself. How damn much he was going to miss her.

She sighed. "It's almost like I'm getting reacquainted with myself."

He smiled. "Well, I hope you like Jenny as much as I do."

A stricken look crossed her face. It was gone almost as quickly, but he'd seen the flicker of pain. He didn't get it. His remark wasn't negative. He had meant to comfort. Did she think it would lead to something else? That he'd beg her to stay?

This chapter in Jen's life was over. That much he got. She needed to go back to the city, back to the work she loved. They'd still be friends. After what they'd been through together, how could they not be? They'd keep in touch, talk on the phone once a week or so in the beginning, but she'd be busy building her new life....

He stood, and she jerked at his abruptness. He had to go. He couldn't stay and let her see how much he wanted to keep her here.

Fear gripped him like a vise. Even if she agreed, it wouldn't work. What if the tumor came back? What if they found another one? What if he let himself love her and something happened?

No way. He couldn't love like that again. It would be too risky. Jenny had to go, and he had to let her.

She got up and faced him. The sadness in her eyes broke his heart. He wanted to run but stayed where he was, his stomach tensing when she touched his cheek. It took all his willpower not to pull her into his arms. That kind of weakness would only prolong the inevitable. Jen would leave, and there wasn't a damn thing he could do about it.

Not a damn thing he should do about it.

"Alex, I don't—" She paused, moistened her lips.

He said nothing, but stared back, expressionless.

She lowered her hand, walked to the radio and turned it off. "I'll start dinner in a couple of hours. I'm going to go lie down."

That seemed sudden. Apprehensive, he studied her

gait. She wasn't limping. "Did you hurt yourself dancing?"

She turned sad eyes to him. "No, dancing didn't hurt me at all."

JENNY FILED the pharmaceutical invoices and organized the clinic's accounts receivable. She had to keep busy or she'd lose it. The new assistant, Cindy, started work tomorrow. Alex had hired her to work full time, which meant there would be little need for Jenny.

That wasn't the only thing that had her distracted and weepy. They hadn't made love in two weeks. Alex always had an excuse, everything short of a damn headache. Plato talked to her more than Alex did these days, and she was pathetically grateful to the bossy bird.

It was getting pretty obvious that Alex wanted her to leave. He never said anything, though. Of course, he didn't have to. His avoidance of her was hint enough.

"Jen?" He walked out of his office with a chart in his hands. The top button of his shirt was undone, and she could see a smattering of light-colored hair.

She wanted to undress him. Lock the clinic door, take the phone off the hook and spend the afternoon making mad passionate love. "Yes?"

"I think I screwed up and booked two appointments for the same time while you went to pick up lunch. Would you check it out for me?"

"Sure." She hid a smile. Damn it, he needed her.

"Oh, and one more thing—"

The clinic door opened, and a young blond woman with a long ponytail gingerly stepped inside.

"Hello, Cindy." Alex greeted her with a warm smile. "I heard you got back from Boston yesterday."

She nodded, her gaze darting to Jenny. She looked so young and nervous. But Alex was easy to work for. He'd put her at ease the first day.

"Have you met Jenny?" he asked, not mentioning she was his wife.

Why should he? In another month or so, she probably wouldn't be his wife anymore. A lump formed in her throat, and she knew she'd have to excuse herself.

"Hi." Cindy gave her a shy smile, then immediately turned to Alex and cringed. "Dr. McAlester, I have to talk to you."

Alex set down the chart. "I hope you aren't nervous about starting tomorrow."

Cindy pressed her lips together, her face starting to turn red. She took a deep breath and blurted, "I won't be coming tomorrow. I can't work here." She sniffed. "I'm really, really sorry, Dr. McAlester. My mom is so mad at me for doing this to you, but I've decided to move to Boston."

"Okay." Surprise flashed across Alex's face. He was displeased, but he didn't show it.

Jenny knew he was upset because of the way he raked a hand through his hair and clenched his fist.

Amazing how well she'd gotten to know his little quirks over the past five months.

She swallowed the dangerous hope that rose in her chest and crowded her throat. He'd need her to fill in until he got someone else. And maybe, in the meantime...

Oh, God, why did she do this to herself? He didn't want her to stay. He would have asked by now. He wouldn't be making it so easy for her to leave.

"I'm so sorry, Dr. McAlester, I really am." The poor young woman looked close to tears.

Alex smiled and crossed the room to put a hand on Cindy's shoulder. "It's okay. I understand."

"Really?"

He nodded, looking so much like the man Jenny had grown to love that her heart ached. Kind. Patient. Understanding. She hadn't seen much of that man in the past month. In fact, she hadn't seen much of him at all.

He chuckled. "Really."

Cindy sighed with relief. "I wish my mom and dad were taking it this well. They think I'm nuts."

Jenny laughed. "That's their job."

They both looked at her in surprise, almost as if they'd forgotten she was there. Or maybe they hadn't expected her to throw in her two cents. She didn't care—she was just too darn happy over this new development. "You should have seen my father's face when I told him I was moving to Boston. You would've thought I'd grown another head."

Cindy's eyes lit with interest. "Were you young then?"

Jenny threw Alex a wounded look that made him grin. "A couple of years older than you are now. I'd just finished community college over in Quincy."

"Did you stay in the city long? My parents think I'll be back before Christmas. But I won't."

Maybe not by Christmas, Jenny thought, but she'd be back. "Long enough."

"Why did you move back *here?*"

Jenny slid a look at Alex. His face was totally expressionless. "Things change. Life changes."

Cindy gave her a puzzled look, then shrugged. "I can't wait. I'm using my graduation money to get an apartment and everything. I know exactly where I want to live." Her youthful exuberance put a knot in Jenny's stomach. "Well, Dr. McAlester..." She placed her hand on the doorknob. "Thanks for not yelling at me."

He chuckled. "Why would I do that?" He lifted his chin. "Go on. You must have a lot of things to do. Have fun in Boston."

Cindy gave him a smile of gratitude, then left.

Alex didn't say anything, just stared at the closed door.

"She'll be back." Jenny finally broke the silence. "Unfortunately, that doesn't help you right now."

He frowned at her. "What makes you think she'll be back?"

"She's young. The grass looks greener in the city." She grinned. "Ironic, isn't it?"

He didn't seem amused. "You were young when you left. You didn't come back."

"I'm here."

An odd hint of disgust crossed his face. "Only because you had to come back. Most of your school friends left, too. You don't see them flocking back." He waved a dismissive hand as if he were bored with the conversation. "But that's neither here nor there."

She stared at him. He was right. Most of the ones who'd left hadn't returned. They were spread out across the country, honing careers or raising children. Her attitude toward Cooper's Corner was different.

He picked up the chart he'd left on the desk. "I have a few calls to make—"

"Alex, wait." She let out a breath. "You don't really have to hire anyone else. I, uh, I've been managing fine alone."

"Of course I do. You're leaving." His voice was so matter-of-fact it broke her heart. "But I was hoping you could give the new person some training before then."

She forced a laugh. "It's not like I'm leaving right away."

His eyes met hers, his expression grim. "Yeah, but you are leaving, Jen."

She shivered. It almost sounded like an ultimatum. God, was he really that sick of her?

He lowered the chart. "I guess now is as good a time as any to bring this up. I know you're probably anxious to get back to New York. I have some money for you. Not a lot but enough to pay for an apartment and living expenses for a few months until you get back on your feet.''

She stared at him, speechless. She understood what he'd said. She just couldn't believe it. Didn't want to believe he was this anxious for her to leave.

"Thank you," she finally said when she could trust her voice not to crack, "but that isn't necessary."

"Consider it a loan, if you want. You can pay me back when the farm sells," Alex said.

She shook her head. She doubted there'd be any money left from the sale of the farm, but that was hardly the point.

"Steven—you remember him? He called last week and gave me a lead on a job." She gave a nonchalant shrug. "I really lucked out. He's even offered me his apartment while he and Brian are in Europe."

Alex blinked. "Great."

She waited for him to say more. He just stood there, that damned expressionless mask in place. She couldn't take it another minute.

"Tell you what," she said, grabbing her purse and keys. "I have an errand to run, and at the same time I'll go put an ad in the paper. I'm sure you won't have trouble finding someone."

"Thanks." At least he had the good grace not to look happy about it. "You don't need to come back. I'll see you at home."

She forced a smile and hurried away before she burst out crying.

"HELLO, JENNY, way to go."

"Shut up, Plato." That bird sounded too much like

Alex. She should have tried doing her exercises in the kitchen, where she wouldn't get any coaching. Or cheerleading. Or reminders that she'd worn out her welcome.

Thinking about her conversation with Alex caused her to misstep. She sank to the floor in defeat. But she wouldn't cry anymore. Not another tear would be wasted. She was well, almost fully recovered, and that was the deal they'd made.

Damn it.

She sniffed and forced herself to her feet.

"Push harder, Jenny."

She glared at Plato. "You have no idea how truly close you are to being thrown in a pot."

"Push harder, Jenny."

She groaned in exasperation, then thought for a moment. Maybe that was the answer. If she pushed hard, too hard, she might set herself back. Have to stay longer. Alex wouldn't throw her out.

Appalled that she'd even entertained the idea for a second, she moved to the couch, stretched out and stared at the ceiling. She'd never pull anything like that. Aside from the ploy being manipulative and pathetic, it wouldn't be fair to Alex. He'd put his life on hold long enough for her.

She closed her eyes, mentally kicking herself. How could she have misread him so badly? She'd convinced herself that his feelings had evolved into love just as hers had.

Sometimes when he watched her—not just when

they were making love, but at odd times, like when they were eating or watching the news—he'd have this tender look on his face that made her think…

Oh, God, why was she doing this to herself? She could analyze his behavior and every facial expression he'd ever made, and it wouldn't change anything. He wanted her gone. For all the tender looks, she'd seen fear, too. It probably scared him witless that he'd never get rid of her.

She opened her eyes, riveting her gaze on the picture of Sara that stood on the mantel. Or maybe he was afraid to let himself feel anything. Jenny's insides tightened. He'd once told her he'd never marry again. Maybe he had developed feelings, and it scared the hell out of him.

She sat up, excitement and hope making her a little light-headed. It was entirely possible. In fact, she'd been rather dense not to have considered the possibility.

"Push harder, Jenny."

She looked at Plato. She'd pushed hard, all right, throughout her whole recovery period. She'd religiously made every physical therapy appointment, persisted in every home exercise, no matter how much she ached, so that her body would get well.

Wasn't her emotional well-being, her chance at love and happiness just as important? Was she so wimpy she'd leave without a fight? Let him look her in the eyes and tell her they had nothing.

She got up and winked at Plato. "You're right. I'm

going to push so hard he'll have to carry me out of here himself.''

ALEX SAT at his desk and stared at his calendar. He had no idea what he'd intended to do next. He'd been distracted all afternoon. Ever since Jen told him she had a lead on a job and an apartment.

So why should it bother him? He wanted her to go, right? She had her life, and he had his. The longer she stayed, the harder it was going to be.

He'd have to have a talk with her before she left and make sure she understood she always had a place to come home to... Except this wasn't her home. Still, if she ever got sick again, or the tumor came back...

The mere idea paralyzed him with fear. He took a deep breath. He'd be careful how he worded the offer, but he had to do it, had to make sure she knew she had a place to come to and get well if she ever got sick again.

The thought unnerved him. He didn't want her in his life because he didn't want to risk loving and losing her. Yet there was no doubt in his mind that if Jen were in trouble, he would want to be by her side no matter what it cost him.

The concept was startling. He picked up the bottle of water he kept on his desk and took a long, cool sip. This didn't make sense. Not one bit. He must be too rattled to think straight.

He set down the water and swore. How could he deny that he already loved her? That the minute she stepped out of his door, he'd experience a loss every bit as great as he had with Sara? Of course Jen would be alive and well and happy somewhere. And he'd be grateful. But that wouldn't fill the void in his heart, the pain of not being able to touch her each day and sleep beside her each night.

He locked his hands behind his head and stared at the ceiling. So now what? He couldn't tell her how he felt. She'd feel obligated to stick around. He couldn't stand that, knowing she wanted to return to the city but was staying out of a sense of obligation.

Damn, how did this get so complicated? How could he have been so stupid as to get emotionally involved? He knew better. Then and now. But that didn't help the heaviness in his heart.

The phone rang, and he was tempted to ignore it. But the clinic was still officially open for another half hour, and besides, it could be Jenny. That possibility had him grabbing the receiver.

"Dr. McAlester? It's Sylvia Samm. I was wondering if I could bring Zeus in tomorrow."

He straightened. "What's wrong with him?"

"Nothing, really. I just wanted to make sure he was healing properly."

Alex relaxed. "Zeus is healed already, Sylvia. He doesn't need a checkup, and frankly, he doesn't need you keeping him penned up like you do." After a lengthy silence, he said, "Sylvia?"

"I'm just worried about him. I don't want him to hurt himself. He's been through enough." She sniffed defensively. "Anyway, I thought you agreed with me."

He scrubbed at his eyes. "I was wrong. Zeus deserves to have as normal a life as possible. Yes, he may hurt himself while getting adjusted, but he'll survive, and he'll be much happier. He can't do that if you're being overprotective."

"I don't understand you, Dr. McAlester. Not at all." She hung up.

Alex sighed. "I don't understand myself," he whispered as he replaced the receiver. That's when he saw her. Jen stood at the door, a smile starting to curve her lips.

"Good advice," she said. "Sounds familiar."

"Okay, so you were right." He watched her walk in and swing around his desk. There was something different about her.

Not physically. Her shiny cinnamon hair was pulled into its usual clip, and she had on the same jeans and T-shirt she wore earlier. But the determination in her eyes, the confidence in her posture put him on alert.

She stopped right beside him and slid a hip onto his desk.

"I've been thinking…" She paused, studying him closely. "I can't leave. I've got to stick around Cooper's Corner." She hesitated, then visibly swallowed. "Otherwise who's going to set you straight when you get off base?"

Her words tumbled in his head as he struggled to understand what she was telling him. She couldn't leave? No. She didn't want to leave. His insides went berserk. He wanted to jump up and grab her. Hold on and never let her go. "I do need advice from time to time."

She nodded sagely, but he could see the flush on her cheeks, the rapid rise and fall of her chest. "You're a great doctor. Smart. Very knowledgeable. But I have to tell you, Doc, your bedside manner needs work."

He let hope flood him. "And you can help with that?"

She nodded, her gaze carefully locked with his. "If you let me."

Alex was too choked up to say anything. He stood and pulled her against him, kissing her hair, her cheek, her lips. "I love you, Jen. I want you to stay with me forever."

She tipped her head to look at him. "Forever is a long time."

"Not long enough, honey."

She pressed her lips together, and he heard her force back a sob. "I love you."

He tightened his arms around her and kissed her. "So, when are we going to start work on that bedside manner?"

EPILOGUE

JENNY EYED the pink-frosted, heart-shaped cake in the magazine and studied her creation with dismay. Darn it. She'd followed the directions to a T. Why didn't her cake look like that?

She sighed. Well, at least you could tell it was a heart. Sort of. The fact that it was Valentine's Day would be a major hint. She shook her head, dropped the magazine in the recycling bin, then hid the cake in the oven.

Alex would be home at any moment. She smiled. He tended to come home earlier on days she didn't work at the clinic. Two years ago when she'd returned to Cooper's Corner she had never dreamed she could be happy living here again, much less being a part-time stay-at-home mom to Plato and Bagel. But there wasn't a place on earth she'd rather be right now.

She heard Alex at the back door and took a deep breath. She'd waited three hours to tell him the news, and she was ready to burst.

"Hi." He smiled, clearly surprised to see her waiting just a few feet away.

"Happy Valentine's Day!"

His smile broadened. "Come here."

She ducked away from him. She knew what would happen next, and it excluded any talking. "Wait. I have a surprise for you."

He caught one of her hands and pulled her toward him. "Let's see." He frowned as if he were thinking hard. "You baked a cake."

She gasped. "Plato told you."

Alex chuckled and touched the tip of her nose. "Pink frosting." He showed her his fingertip. "Dead giveaway."

"Darn it." She rubbed her nose. "Anyway, that's not the surprise."

"What is it?"

"Guess."

"Jen, you know I hate that...."

She laughed. "I went to the doctor today."

His expression tensed. "And?"

"You know how Phyllis and Maureen have been telling me I should do some part-time business consulting?" The fear on his face prompted her to cut the teasing. "Well, I won't have time. The doctor gave his okay for us to start a family."

Alex's expression lightened by degrees as the news registered. "Ah, Jen." He wrapped his arms around her waist and picked her up off the floor. "I love you."

She choked back a sob. He was the most loving, patient, incredible man she'd ever met, and now she could give him something precious. "Tell me again after you try the cake."

*Welcome to Twin Oaks—
the new B and B in Cooper's Corner,
Massachusetts. Bed and breakfast will
never be the same!*

COOPER'S CORNER
*a new Harlequin continuity series
Continues June 2003 with
HER STOLEN PAST
by Amanda Stevens*

*Librarian Beth Young was so quiet, she
simply blended into the town of Cooper's
Corner. But Clint Cooper, co-owner of the
Twin Oaks, couldn't help but notice her as
she played piano each evening at the B and
B. Her music was haunting…and to Clint,
so was her beauty. But Beth didn't dare act
on the attraction she felt for Clint.*

Here's a preview!

CHAPTER ONE

"ANY OF THIS JOG your memory?" MacMillan queried.

Beth shook her head.

"Didn't think so." He closed the briefcase and stood. "Well, I guess that's all we can do for now. We'll be in touch. And in the meantime, if you get your memory back, you call us."

He moved away from the bed, but before he got to the door, he turned as if an idea had suddenly dawned on him. He took a step toward her. "Oh, and one other thing you should know. The man who pulled you from the river that night said he saw two sets of headlights on the mountain. One set was lower to the ground, presumably on your car. The other lights looked as if they were on a truck or SUV. He said for a few seconds the two sets of lights were traveling side by side down the mountain. Then your car went into a spin and slid over the side. He had the impression that you may have been forced over."

She gasped. "You mean someone...tried to kill me?"

"We don't know for sure what happened. All we can do is speculate. It's been my experience, though, that women don't usually go out alone in the dead of night—much less in a driving rainstorm—just for the hell of it. Something happened on that mountain. You were running from something. Or someone. I'd stake my life on it."

A .38 special, serial number completely filed away. Two rounds missing from the clip.

Ten thousand dollars. Small denominations.

You were running from something. Or someone.

"Do I need a lawyer?" she asked hoarsely.

MacMillan seemed surprised by the question. "We don't even have evidence that a crime has been committed, unless you know something we don't. But then, even if you did, you wouldn't remember it, would you?" Something she could only name as suspicion gleamed in his eyes, making her tremble even more.

I didn't do anything, she wanted to tell him, but how could she know that for sure? How could she defend herself when she didn't know who she was or what kind of person she'd been? Was she capable of violence? Deception? Betrayal? She had no idea.

As if reading the terror and confusion in her eyes, the detective nodded. "Quite a predicament, isn't it? If someone did try to kill you on that mountain and he finds out you're still alive, he could come looking for you. And if Marsden and I find out you stole that money or used that gun, *we'll* come looking for you." His gaze hardened. "Either way, I'd say you're in one hell of a mess."

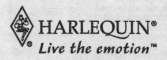

COOPER'S CORNER

FREE Bathroom Accessories
With proofs of purchase
from Cooper's Corner titles.

YES! Please send me my FREE bathroom accessory without cost or obligation, except for shipping and handling.

In U.S., mail to:	In CANADA, mail to:
COOPER'S CORNER	**COOPER'S CORNER**
P.O. Box 9047	P.O. Box 613
Buffalo, NY	Fort Erie, ON
14269-9047	L2A 5X3

_____

Name (PLEASE PRINT)

_____

Address   Apt. #

_____

City   State/Prov.   Zip/Postal Code

Enclosed are three (3) proofs of purchase from three (3) different Cooper's Corner titles and $1.50 shipping and handling, for the first item, $0.50 for each additional item selected.

Please specify which item(s) you would like to receive:

- ❏   Liquid Soap Dispenser
- ❏   Soap Dish
- ❏   Toothbrush Holder
- ❏   Drinking Cup

FREE BATHROOM ACCESSORY TERMS

To receive your free bathroom accessory (estimated retail value $30.00 for complete set), complete the above order form. Mail it to us with three proofs of purchase per accessory chosen, one of which can be found in the right-hand corner of this page. Requests must be received no later than October 31, 2003. Your Cooper's Corner Bathroom Accessory costs you only $1.50 shipping and handling for the first item selected, $0.50 for each additional selection. N.Y. state residents must add applicable sales tax on shipping and handling charge. **Please allow 6-8 weeks for receipt of order. Offer good in Canada and U.S. only.**
Offer good while quantities last. Offer limited to one per household.

COOPER'S
CORNER
ONE PROOF
OF PURCHASE
ccpop

When duty calls...
love answers!

Top Harlequin
Intrigue® authors

JOANNA
WAYNE

B.J.
DANIELS

WHEN DUTY CALLS

Two full-length novels.

There's nothing more
irresistible than a red-blooded,
strong-willed lawman who
protects and rescues—and
this volume brings two
of them...for hours of
reading pleasure!

Pick up WHEN DUTY CALLS—
available in July 2003.

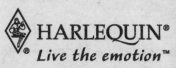

HARLEQUIN®
Live the emotion™

Visit us at www.eHarlequin.com   BR2WDC

Welcome to Twin Oaks—
the new B and B in Cooper's Corner.
Some come for pleasure, others for passion—
and one to set things straight...

Three brothers, one
tuxedo...and one destiny!

*Date
With
Destiny*

A brand-new anthology from
USA TODAY bestselling author
KRISTINE ROLOFSON
MURIEL JENSEN
KRISTIN GABRIEL

The package said "R. Perez" and
inside was a tuxedo. But which
Perez brother—Rick, Rafe or
Rob—was it addressed to? This
tuxedo is on a mission...to lead
each of these men to the altar!

DATE WITH DESTINY
will introduce you to
the characters of
Forrester Square...
an exciting new continuity
starting in August 2003.

Forrester Square
LEGACIES . LIES . LOVE .

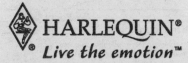
HARLEQUIN®
Live the emotion™

Visit us at www.eHarlequin.com

PHDWD